MANDIE
AND THE
MEDICINE
MAN

Mandie Mysteries

9709

MANDIE
AND THE
MEDICINE
MAN

Lois Gladys Leppard

BETHANY HOUSE PUBLISHERS
MINNEAPOLIS, MINNESOTA 55438

Library of Congress Catalog Card Number 85-73426

ISBN 0-87123-891-8

Published by Bethany House Publishers ·
A Division of Bethany Fellowship, Inc.
6820 Auto Club Road, Minneapolis, Minnesota 55438

Printed in the United States of America

About the Author

LOIS GLADYS LEPPARD has been a Federal Civil Service employee in various countries around the world. She makes her home in South Carolina.

The stories of her own mother's childhood are the basis for many of the incidents incorporated in this series.

Contents

With love to all those wonderful readers
who have written to me, including:

Angela
Julia Batson
Amanda Berl
Katie Bolding
Amy, Robyn & Angel Booth
Stephanie Brock
Michelle & Malissa Burns
Christy Cook
Danielle & Deeann Cowan
Melanie Cox
Aaron Crabb
Heather & Jennifer Crowe
Deanne Devlin
Linda D'Hoore
Colleen Dorr
Renee Fowler
Megan Frahm
Karen Garner
Anna Gilbertson
Kristi Gosnell
Carolyn Grant
Ashley Hall
Krista, Alicia & Sara Hanson
Jennifer Hinson
Mary Hoffman
Melissa Holden
Amanda Howard
Mariah Hutchison
Samara & Nicky Ibanez
Julie Jackson
Amy Karcich
L. Vande Krol
Krista Kulp
Cindy & Candy Leapord

Lisa Lee
Jennifer Lewis
Jennifer Little
Margaret Long
Christi Mc Croskey
Lashon & Sonya Miner
Melissa Mitchell
Kelly Morris
Mandy Nesbitt
Ruby Newton
Lisa Nygren
Jennifer Owens
Kimberly Reeves
Nancy Pafford-Reifenstein
Jessica Robinson
Tobey Roethler
Karin Schorr
Michael Schroeder
Ella Severs
Georgia Shelton
Sandra & Stephanie Springer
Malinda Stiver
Barbie Stufflebeam
Nellie Suber
Debbie Summerall
Anne Telker
Rochelle TerMaat
Tanya Turcotte
Michelle Van Mill
Angie Wallace
Gretchen Walters
Margaret Watson
Jackie Wessels
Mindy Wilson

Chapter 1 / Off for the Holidays

"I wish you could come home with me," Mandie told Celia as they packed their trunks.

All the students at Misses Heathwood's School for Girls in Asheville, North Carolina, were getting ready to leave for their first holidays of the school year.

"I wanted you to go to Charleston with us." Mandie's blue eyes sparkled. "I can't wait to see the ocean!"

"Mandie, you know I'm torn between this wonderful trip you have planned and going home to see my mother," Celia answered. She folded a dress and laid it in the open trunk. "It would be nice if I could do both, but I can't. You know I haven't seen my mother since I came to school here. I've just got to go home."

Mandie straightened up from the trunk she was packing and studied her friend with the sad green eyes and thick, curly auburn hair. "I know," she agreed. "That's what you should do. This will be a short holiday anyway. Just one week. Maybe you can come home with me for Thanksgiving. We'll get two whole weeks then."

"I'll see," Celia replied. "My Aunt Rebecca should be here pretty soon. She'll spend the night here at the school, and we'll leave tomorrow morning to go home to Richmond. It'll be good to get home again, see my mother, and the horses, and my dog, Prickles."

"I'm glad my mother took Snowball home with her when she and Uncle John were here last week. It has been nice having my kitten right here in town at my grandmother's house. But since Grandmother is going away on a long trip, Snowball wouldn't be able to stay there any longer," Mandie said.

"When do you leave?" Celia asked.

"Mother and Uncle John ought to be here early tomorrow morning, and then we'll leave on the train," Mandie replied. "We'll spend tomorrow night at home in Franklin, and then the next day we'll start out for Charleston. I'm so glad Tommy Patton's parents invited us to his home there. I can't believe that the time has finally come to go."

Suddenly there was a knock at the door of their room. When Mandie opened the door, Aunt Phoebe, the old Negro who worked for the school, was standing there.

"Missy, Miz Hope want you down to de office," the black woman told Mandie.

"Miss Hope? Oh, goodness! What have I done now?" Mandie gasped, dropping the skirt she held. "Aunt Phoebe, what does she want?"

"Don't you be gittin' all flustered, Missy," said Aunt Phoebe. "Miz Hope, she don't seem upset 'tall. De doctuh man he be in huh office."

"Dr. Woodard? He's in Miss Hope's office? Goodness, I'd better go see what she wants!" Mandie exclaimed.

As Mandie ran out the door, Celia called to her. "Hurry back and tell me what's going on."

Mandie quickly made her way to Miss Hope's office

on the main floor. The door was open. Dr. Woodard sat in front of Miss Hope's desk. Miss Hope, smoothing back a stray lock of faded auburn hair, smiled at Mandie as she entered.

"Dr. Woodard, is anything wrong?" Mandie asked anxiously.

"No, no, Amanda. Nothing serious," Miss Hope told her quietly. "Sit down for a minute."

Mandie sat in the other chair and looked from Miss Hope to the doctor.

Dr. Woodard cleared his throat. "Amanda, your mother and your Uncle John will not be coming for you tomorrow—" he began.

"Not coming for me?" Mandie broke in quickly.

"No. You see, I had to come here to Asheville to see some patients and will be going home myself on the train tomorrow," the doctor explained, "so you're to go back with me to Franklin."

"Oh, that's great! I was afraid something was wrong," Mandie responded, a smile lighting up her blue eyes.

"Well, there is a little change in plans," the doctor said slowly. "You see, you probably won't be going on to Charleston the next day."

Tears filled Mandie's eyes. "We aren't going to Charleston, Dr. Woodard? Why not? Tommy's family is expecting us."

"Amanda, please let Dr. Woodard explain without any more interruptions," Miss Hope reprimanded her.

"I'm sorry, Miss Hope, Dr. Woodard," Mandie apologized.

Dr. Woodard looked at her with concern. "We're having some trouble at the hospital," he said.

"Oh, no!" Mandie gasped.

"Someone is tearing down the walls of the hospital as fast as they're being put up," the doctor explained. "So far, we have no idea who would do such a thing, but I told your Uncle John you'd want to come and help solve the mystery, isn't that right?"

"Well, yes, Dr. Woodard." Mandie hesitated. "But I would like to go to Charleston, too."

"Your Uncle John said that as soon as this matter is cleared up, you will all go on to Charleston as planned. Maybe it won't take long. We've already put guards around the place," he said.

Miss Hope sat forward. "This is the hospital for the Cherokees that is being built with the gold you and your friends found in a cave, isn't it, Amanda?" she asked.

"Yes, ma'am," Mandie replied. "The great Cherokee warrior, Tsali, left the gold in a cave. After we found the gold, the Cherokees refused to have anything to do with it. They said it would cause bad luck. So they put me in charge of the gold, asking me to use it for whatever I saw fit. I knew they needed a hospital, so we're building one for them."

"That is a big job for a twelve-year-old girl, but it's a sensible thing for you to do, Amanda," the school-mistress told her. "I do hope you get all this straightened out."

"I hope it won't take long." Amanda looked at Dr. Woodard, pleading. "I want to go to Charleston. I've never seen the ocean, and I've been so excited about this trip," she said.

"We'll all pitch in, Amanda," Dr. Woodard promised. "The Cherokees will help us solve this thing, and I'm sure you'll get to Charleston." He stood and patted her blonde head. "Just be sure you're ready when I call for you tomorrow morning so we can make the train on time."

"I'll be ready." Mandie got up and hurried to the door. "I'd better finish my packing. See you in the morning, Dr. Woodard."

Racing up the steps to the room she shared with Celia Hamilton on the third floor, Mandie burst through the door. Celia stopped packing and looked up.

"I'm going home with Dr. Woodard tomorrow," Mandie told her friend. "Somebody is tearing down the Cherokees' hospital as fast as it's being built. I have to go home and stop them."

Celia smiled. "You? Stop them?"

"Sure. Joe, and Sallie, and Dimar will all help me. When we work on a mystery we always solve it one way or another." Mandie laughed, walking around the room. "Of course it usually takes some grown-ups to help. But we'll have to hurry and solve this mystery so we can go on to Charleston before we use up all the holidays."

"I do hope you're able to visit Charleston," Celia said. "I know how much you want to go."

There was another knock at the door. Aunt Phoebe once again brought a message.

"Message fo' you dis time, Missy Celia," said the old woman. "Dat ahnt of yours be waitin' downstairs wid Miz Hope. She say fo' you to git right down."

"Thanks, Aunt Phoebe," Celia said, following her into the hallway. "I'll be right back, Mandie."

Mandie continued packing. In a few minutes Celia was back, bringing a tiny dark-haired lady with her.

"Aunt Rebecca, this is Amanda Shaw—Mandie I call her. She's my best friend," Celia introduced them. "Mandie, this is my Aunt Rebecca."

"How do you do, Miss ... ah ... Miss ..." Mandie

stopped and smiled at the woman. Turning to Celia, she asked, "Well, what is her name? I can't call her Aunt Rebecca, you know."

The woman reached out and took Mandie's small hand in hers. "Of course you can, dear," the lady said. "My name is Rebecca Hamilton. I'm Celia's father's sister. I've heard so much about you from letters Celia has written to her mother. I feel I know you. Now, what can I do to help you girls get finished?"

"Nothing, Aunt Rebecca. Just sit over there in that chair and talk to us while we get done." Celia motioned toward the only empty chair in the littered room. "How is Mother? I was hoping she could come with you so she could meet Mandie and see the school."

"I know, dear, but she wasn't feeling up to the trip. I doubt that the school has changed much since she was a student here," Aunt Rebecca said, relaxing in the chair. She turned to Mandie. "I know she would like to meet Elizabeth's daughter, however. She told me that your mother went to school here with her."

"My mother is not coming either," Mandie said. "Dr. Woodard is in town, and I'll be going home to Franklin as he goes tomorrow." She told Aunt Rebecca what was happening at the hospital.

"I think it's wonderful for you to do such a thing, building a hospital for those poor Indians," the woman replied.

"Well, after all, they are my kinpeople. My grandmother was full-blooded Cherokee," Mandie explained, continuing to fill her trunk.

"Yes, I believe I remember hearing about that. Your father died and then your mother married his brother, John Shaw, didn't she?" Aunt Rebecca asked.

"Yes, ma'am," Mandie said sadly as she pushed back her long blonde hair. "My father was a wonderful man. I loved him so much. Of course I love Uncle John, too, but no one can replace my father."

"I know that from experience, Amanda," Aunt Rebecca replied. "My father died when I was small. My mother never remarried."

"I can just barely remember Grandmother Hamilton," Celia said. "Mandie, you're lucky your Grandmother Taft is still living. My mother and Aunt Rebecca are all the close relatives I have left."

"I have lots of Cherokee relatives. There must be dozens and dozens of them. But then the Indians claim kinship with each other whether they're really blood related or not," Mandie explained.

Aunt Rebecca smiled. "In a sense that's true, isn't it? God made us all. We're really all brothers and sisters," she said.

Mandie and Celia nodded thoughtfully.

"So, now you're going home and then on to see your Cherokee relatives before you make this trip to Charleston. I wish you a lot of luck with the hospital. I hope they catch whoever is responsible for such vandalism."

The bell in the backyard rang loudly for supper, and the girls stopped working.

"Aunt Rebecca, let me show you to the guest room downstairs," Celia said. "We have only about ten minutes before we have to be in the dining room, and I know you want to freshen up. Be right back, Mandie."

"I'll see you downstairs, Miss-Aunt Rebecca." Mandie smiled.

"Yes, dear," the lady replied, hurrying out the door with Celia.

In a couple of minutes Celia was back, and the girls rushed to the bathroom down the hall to wash their hands. As they came back out into the hallway, they almost ran into April Snow.

Mandie looked up into the tall girl's face. "April, I'm sorry you won't be able to go home for the holidays," she said kindly.

"Whether I go home or not is my own business," April snapped. "Just be sure and remember that."

Mandie and Celia looked at each other as April rushed on down the hallway.

"She just won't let anyone be nice to her," Mandie said.

Celia frowned. "April's not very nice to be nice to," she said. "That girl is always making trouble. You know that as well as I do."

"I sure do," Mandie agreed. "But don't forget. The Bible says to return good for evil."

"It'd sure take a whole lot of good to even things out with her evil," Celia said.

"We should keep on trying though," Mandie reminded her.

After the evening meal, the girls hurriedly left the dining room.

Just outside the door, April Snow stepped in front of them. "Enjoy your holidays because you might not enjoy coming back," she sneered. Turning quickly, she disappeared down the hallway.

"Now, what on earth can she be talking about?" Mandie asked in surprise.

"She's talking about making trouble, and we are her target," Celia replied.

"Well, we'll see about that," said Mandie.

Back in their room the two girls thought the night would never end. Excited about their forthcoming trips, they talked most of the night away. Then before daylight they got up, dressed, and waited for the bell to ring for breakfast.

The morning meal with Miss Prudence, the head schoolmistress, watching over them seemed to take longer than usual. Neither Mandie nor Celia could eat much.

When it was time to leave, Uncle Cal, Aunt Phoebe's husband, brought the girls' trunks downstairs and loaded them into the school rig. While they waited on the veranda, Dr. Woodard arrived, and Mandie introduced him to Aunt Rebecca.

The two adults stood chatting while Mandie and Celia went back inside to bid Miss Hope good-bye.

"We are leaving now, Miss Hope," Mandie said as they stood before the schoolmistress's desk.

"You're both leaving?" Miss Hope looked surprised. "But you are going in opposite directions, Amanda."

"Dr. Woodard said we'd just all go to the depot together," Mandie explained. "Celia's train will come through about thirty minutes ahead of ours. So we can save Uncle Cal another trip to the station."

Miss Hope stood up, walked around the desk, and put an arm around each girl. "I know it's just for a few days, but I'm going to miss you both," she said. "Be good girls and tell me about your trips when you get back."

"We will, Miss Hope," they promised.

April Snow caught up with the two girls in the hallway. She stepped in front of them, blocking their way to the front door.

"Just remember what I said," April threatened. "Enjoy your trips because you might not enjoy coming back."

"Just what do you mean?" Mandie asked.

"Just what I said," April replied. "You'll see when you get back."

Stepping around them, April headed down the hallway in the other direction.

Mandie and Celia looked at each in exasperation.

"I wish she wouldn't act like that," Mandie complained. "It sort of puts a damper on things. Now I'll be wondering the whole time I'm gone what she's talking about."

"Me, too," Celia agreed.

When Mandie and Celia rejoined Dr. Woodard and Aunt Rebecca on the veranda, Uncle Cal was waiting for them in the rig. Climbing aboard, the girls began talking excitedly about being free for a whole week.

Not long after they arrived at the depot, a big, noisy train came whistling up the track. The girls looked at each other.

"I'm going to miss you, Celia, but I hope you have a nice time at home with your mother," Mandie said, giving her friend a hug.

"I'll be thinking about you, Mandie, and wondering how your trip is turning out," Celia replied. "I hope you catch those culprits real fast so you can go to Charleston."

The train came to a halt and sat there puffing.

"Come, Celia. Good-bye, Amanda," Aunt Rebecca called to them. She turned to board the train, letting Celia go ahead of her. "Good day, Dr. Woodard. It was nice meeting you."

"My pleasure, ma'am," said Dr. Woodard, removing his hat. "Give my regards to Celia's mother."

Celia quickly found a seat near an open window and

waved to Mandie. As the train hustled on its way, the wind blew Celia's auburn curls around her bonnet.

Mandie waved until the train disappeared down the track. Then she turned to Dr. Woodard. "I hope our train isn't late. I'm in a hurry to get home and catch those crooks," she said. "If it takes too long, I won't be able to go to Charleston. And I've just got to see the ocean."

"Don't worry, Amanda. I think you'll make it," Dr. Woodard told her. "We'll all help."

The train was on time. Mandie and Dr. Woodard were soon on their way to Franklin.

Chapter 2 / Home Again!

The train slowly chugged into Franklin, and stopped with a big sigh. Instantly, Mandie was already out of her seat. She looked out the window for her mother or Uncle John. There was no one on the platform that she knew.

"Doctor Woodard, I don't see Mother or Uncle John," she said anxiously.

Dr. Woodard rose to join her. "No, I'm supposed to take you home. I told them it wasn't necessary to meet the train," the doctor said. "Come on. I'll get my horse and buggy from the livery stable. Then we'll come back and get the luggage. Joe is at your mother's house, and I'll be staying there tonight, too. They're all getting ready for the journey tomorrow to the Cherokee hospital."

"Now don't tell me Joe's school is having another holiday. They've already had their harvest break," Mandie said, hurrying down the steps onto the platform.

"Yes, a whole week, just like you," Dr. Woodard replied, leading the way down the street to the livery stable.

"He must not go to school as much as I do then. We didn't have a break for harvest when he did," Mandie protested.

"No, but he goes longer into the summer. Don't you remember? You went to school with him when you lived with your father at Charley Gap," the old man reminded her.

"But he's in a higher school this year. It's not the same school we went to together," she explained.

"Come to think of it, you're right," Dr. Woodard agreed. "Well, here we are."

As they entered the wide doorway of the livery stable, the owner came to meet them. He had already harnessed Dr. Woodard's horse to the buggy and brought it out.

"Heard the train come in. Knew you'd be in a hurry," the man told Dr. Woodard.

"That's a mighty thoughtful thing for you to do, Charles. Thank you," said the doctor, taking the reins. "Climb in, Amanda."

On the short trip home, Mandie eagerly looked all around her. Having been away at school, she had missed everyone in Franklin. She waved to people she knew as they passed on the street. It was exciting to be home.

Dr. Woodard reined in the horses at the hitching post in front of the Shaws' big house.

Joe came running down the walkway to meet them. "Mandie, welcome home!" he cried, reaching out to help her down from the buggy.

Holding his hand tightly, Mandie thought for a moment, *Should I slowly descend from the buggy like a lady, the way the school teaches, or should I be myself?*

Joe looked up at her to see why she was hesitating.

Mandie smiled and jumped down from the buggy. It was nice to be able to be Mandie Shaw again, not the stiff lady the school was trying to make her into.

"Oh, Joe, I'm so glad you're here," she said, "even though I think you get more holidays than I do," she added slyly.

"But I really work hard at school and learn something worthwhile," Joe defended himself. "We don't have all that extra baloney they're teaching you."

"I'd much rather go to school with you. You know that," Mandie said. "But Mother insists I go to the school where she went." Mandie started toward the house.

There, on the veranda, everyone was waiting for her: Aunt Lou, the housekeeper, her enormous black face beaming, Liza, the young Negro maid who was also Mandie's friend, Jennie, the cook, Jason Bond, the caretaker, and of course her mother and Uncle John.

Snowball, her white kitten, bounded toward her, meowing loudly. Mandie grabbed him and broke into a run to the porch, pulling off her bonnet as she ran.

She embraced each one amid their welcoming remarks.

"My child, I'se so glad to see you back," said Aunt Lou, smoothing Mandie's long blonde hair.

"Aunt Lou, I've missed you so much," Mandie told her. She turned to Jennie. "I sure hope you've got something good cooked. That school food is not half as good as yours, Jennie."

"I got a lil' bit o' ev'ything all hot and waitin'," Jennie replied.

"Mr. Jason, I hope you haven't let anyone into our secret tunnel," said Mandie to the caretaker.

"It's locked up and I'm the one that's got the key," said Jason Bond, his gray eyes twinkling.

Mandie grabbed Liza's hand. "Liza, just wait till you hear about that school!" she exclaimed.

"Is it dat bad, Missy?" the Negro girl asked.

Mandie glanced at her mother, then bent forward and whispered in the girl's ear. "I'll tell you how bad later."

Liza grinned and danced around the porch.

"Mother, Uncle John, it's so good to be home," Mandie said, embracing her mother and tiptoeing to kiss her uncle's cheek.

"Enjoy it, dear," Elizabeth Shaw told her daughter. "We have to leave early tomorrow morning to go to Deep Creek."

"Deep Creek? Are we going to stay at Uncle Ned's house?" Mandie asked.

"Yes, the hospital site is nearer his house than the others," said Uncle John, "and he's expecting us."

"Good." Mandie grinned. "That means I'll get to see Sallie and Morning Star."

"Right now I think we'd better get inside and finish things up for our journey," her mother said.

Joe stepped to Mandie's side. "I'm going with you to Uncle Ned's," he said.

"And I'll be along out there later after I make some calls here in Franklin," Dr. Woodard added.

Mandie could hardly contain her excitement. "This is going to be a great trip," she said, swinging her bonnet by its ribbon.

Mandie spent a happy evening with her family and friends. When she told Liza about the "uppity" school she was attending, Liza laughed till her sides hurt.

"Lawsy mercy, Missy," Liza gasped, dancing around Mandie's bedroom. "Why don' you come home and go to school with yo' own kind o' people? Whut good all dat fancy schoolin' gonna do you when you gonna wind up marryin' dat Joe boy?"

Mandie blushed. "Liza! My mother went to that school, and she married my father who was half Cherokee. And Uncle John is half Cherokee, too, of course, since he's my father's brother."

"Well, maybe Joe boy will git to be a rich man somehow," Liza said. "But he don' need no money if he marries you 'cause yo' uncle de richest man dis side o' Richmond. And lawsy mercy, dey say yo' mother got money to burn."

"Better not let Aunt Lou hear you say that. Remember?" Mandie warned her. "She won't like you discussing people's business."

"Whut she don't know can't hurt her," Liza laughed. "Well, anyhow I gotta go. See you in de mornin'."

"Good night, Liza," said Mandie.

"Night, Missy," Liza replied. "I knows you gonna sleep good in yo' own bed."

"You bet." Mandie hopped into bed as Liza slipped out into the hallway.

The world was going around in Mandie's pretty blonde head as it touched the pillow. So much was happening. And she didn't want to sleep too much of her holidays away.

Morning came and Elizabeth was shaking her to wake up.

"Darling, it's time to get up," Elizabeth told her.

Startled awake, Mandie sat up and looked around for a second before she realized where she was. Then she jumped quickly out of bed, dumping Snowball onto the floor from his place at the foot of her bed.

"Good morning, Mother. I'm so glad to be home," Mandie said, stretching and yawning.

"I'm glad to have you home with us for a while," Elizabeth told her, giving her a quick hug. "Now wear some serviceable clothes on the road, dear. It'll be a long, dusty journey. You've been there before. You know how it is."

"Yes, ma'am," Mandie replied. "I'll wear my red calico and take the blue gingham."

"That'll be fine. Now hurry and dress," her mother urged.

"Mother, would you mind if I took Sallie and Morning Star some presents?" Mandie asked.

"Why, no, dear. That would be nice," Elizabeth replied. "What would you like to give them?"

Reaching into a bureau drawer where she had unpacked her things, Mandie pulled out an ivory fan. "How about this for Morning Star?" she asked.

"Well, I suppose so. I don't know whether she'd have any use for it, but give it to her if you like," Elizabeth told her.

Then Mandie held up a small velvet-covered Bible. "And this for Sallie? I bought it in Asheville for myself, but I have the Bible that you gave me. I don't really need this one, too."

"I know Sallie would appreciate that," her mother agreed. "Now do hurry, dear."

"I will, Mother," Mandie promised. "The sooner we get to Deep Creek, the sooner we'll get our job done, and the sooner we can go to Charleston."

Elizabeth laughed. "I suppose that makes sense," she said, leaving the room.

As soon as they all finished breakfast, Dr. Woodard left to make his calls, and Mandie, Elizabeth, Uncle John, and Joe climbed into the big covered wagon. All the others gathered on the veranda to see them off.

Mandie carefully tucked her presents for Sallie and

Morning Star into a bag and then sat down beside Joe at the back of the wagon.

Snowball curled up in Mandie's lap as they traveled quickly down the rocky dirt road. The mountainous terrain bounced the wagon around, uphill and downhill. As the wagon swayed far to the right and then far to the left, Mandie and Joe held on to the side rails of the wagon. Snowball sank his claws into Mandie's apron to keep from sliding around.

When Mandie and Joe tried to talk, their voices trembled from the vibration of the rough road.

After a long time the road became parallel to the Tuckasegee River. Then they crossed an old wooden bridge and traveled along the rocky banks of Deep Creek. The glistening water flowed over hundreds of rocks on the clear bottom.

"Look!" Mandie cried, pointing to the creek. "Wouldn't I—"

"Don't say it!" Joe interrupted. "I know you'd like to get in that water, but remember the last time we traveled along this road and you decided to put your feet in the water?"

"I know, I know," Mandie replied. "I remember that awful panther staring at me! And Tsa'ni wouldn't help me. If Uncle Ned hadn't come along right then, I might not be here now to tell about it. That panther was ready to come after me."

Joe reached for her hand. "I don't understand Tsa'ni," he said. "He's your cousin, but he tries to see how mean he can be."

"That's because he's full Cherokee and I'm only one-fourth." Mandie sighed. "And he doesn't like white people," she added.

"Well, he'd better behave himself this time," Joe said. "Or I'll see to it that he wishes he had."

Mandie looked at Joe and didn't answer. She remembered all the trouble Tsa'ni had caused on their other trip to Deep Creek.

Cornfields with bare dried-up stalks began appearing along the way. Harvest came early in the North Carolina mountains. The odor of food cooking over wood fires filled their nostrils.

The wagon rounded a sharp bend in the road. Several log cabins came into view.

"We're here!" Mandie cried, trying to lean out and see ahead of the wagon. Snowball fell off her lap. He stretched and started washing his white fur.

Joe grabbed the edge of Mandie's apron. "Mandie, be careful! You'll fall out!" he warned her.

Mandie sat down quickly. "Oh, well, we're almost to Uncle Ned's house anyway."

Chapter 3 / Visit with Uncle Ned

John Shaw slowed the wagon in front of the largest cabin. The house looked very similar to the one in which Mandie had lived with her father until he died. The old cabin was made of logs chinked together and had a huge rock chimney at one end. The door stood open. Horses grazed behind a split-rail fence.

After the wagon came to a halt by the barn, John helped Elizabeth down. Mandie, with Snowball on her shoulder, jumped off the wagon with Joe.

Her father's Indian friend, Uncle Ned, and his wife, Morning Star, and their granddaughter, Sallie, stood waiting by the open door to greet them.

"Welcome!" said Uncle Ned with a big smile.

"Hello, Uncle Ned," Mandie replied, reaching up to hug his neck. Then she embraced the old Indian woman who stood beside him, grinning. "Morning Star, I'm so glad to see you." Reaching out to their granddaughter, she cried excitedly, "Oh, Sallie, I have so much to tell you!"

"And I have things to tell you," Sallie replied, pushing her long black hair back with a toss of her head.

"Come," Uncle Ned said, leading them all into the cabin.

Joe quickly helped Uncle John bring the bags in from the wagon, and Mandie retrieved the presents she had brought.

Inside, Morning Star removed a cloth from a long, rough, wooden table, revealing dishes piled high with steaming, delicious-smelling food, all ready for supper.

Mandie looked around. Everything was the same. At the far end of the room were several beds built into the wall and covered with cornshuck mattresses. Curtains hanging between the beds could be pulled around each one for privacy. Over in the other corner stood a spinning wheel and a loom. And against the wall was a ladder going upstairs, where there were more beds in the two rooms there.

Mandie walked over to Morning Star with the ivory fan in her hand. "Morning Star, I brought you a present," Mandie told her. Spreading the fan wide, she fanned herself with it, and then handed it, closed, to the old woman.

Morning Star looked at the fan, puzzled. Then she managed to open it and stood there fanning her smiling face.

"Good!" Morning Star grunted. She couldn't speak English, but she could understand some things.

Mandie turned to Sallie and handed her the velvet-covered Bible.

Sallie fingered it excitedly. "This is for me?" she asked.

"Yes, I bought it in Asheville," Mandie told her.

"Thank you, thank you, Mandie!" Sallie cried, hugging her friend. Sallie showed the Bible to Morning Star, talking rapidly in Cherokee.

Then Morning Star gave Mandie a big hug, fanning

herself all the while with her new ivory fan.

"She thanks you," Sallie explained. "She hopes we soon find the crooks who are tearing down the hospital."

"Thank you," Mandie told the old woman.

Uncle Ned, standing nearby, seemed proud to have the white people in his house. He and Morning Star had once lived in the house of Mandie's grandparents, and he tried hard to do things the way his guests expected.

"Wash! Eat!" Uncle Ned said loudly. "Food get cold."

John and Elizabeth headed for the washpan on the shelf. A clean towel hung on a nail beside it. A bucketful of fresh drinking water sat nearby with a gourd dipper hanging on a nail above it. As soon as John and Elizabeth washed their faces and hands, Joe and Mandie did likewise.

"Come on, Joe," Sallie said, leading him to the side of the table opposite where the adults were seated. "I will sit between you and Mandie so I can talk to both of you."

"I sure hope you're not having owl stew again," Joe moaned as he sat down.

"Why, Joe, I thought you liked owl stew," Mandie teased.

Sallie smiled. "You are lucky; my grandmother has cooked ham tonight. Can you not smell it?" the Indian girl asked, straightening her full, red flowered skirt as she sat down.

"Hmm," Joe sniffed. "Well, yeh, but I was afraid it was something else that might smell like ham. And I'm so hungry I could eat almost anything—except owl stew."

Uncle Ned stood at the head of the table and tapped his tin plate. "John Shaw will thank Big God for food," the old Indian announced.

They all bowed their heads as John returned thanks.

"Thank you, dear God, for the privilege of being with our dear friends again, and for the good food you have supplied for this meal that we are about to partake of. And, dear God, please lead us and guide us in our search for those who are tearing down the hospital the Cherokees so badly need. And, dear God, please give us the courage and strength to follow through with this and get the hospital built. We ask your blessing on everyone present at this table. Amen."

Joe looked at the two girls. "Now that's what we came for. We've got to get that hospital built," he said as the adults began their own conversation.

"You are right, Joe," Sallie agreed. "We must find out who is tearing down the walls and put a stop to it."

"Yes, Sallie," Mandie said. "We're all going to see what's being done there. I haven't even seen the land cleared for it, much less the building, because I've been away at that silly school."

Sallie passed Joe a big platter of ham. "Please, tell me about your school, Mandie," she begged. "Why do you call it silly?"

Joe took several large slices of ham, then helped himself to the potatoes sitting in front of him and passed the bowl to the girls.

Mandie, helping herself, explained. "They teach you to be what they call *a lady*. It's a lot of put-on and silly stuff. You learn how to walk with a book balanced on your head so you'll be straight. You learn how to stoop and pick up something without sticking your bottom up in the air. You learn how to talk quietly, in what they call a *well-modulated voice*. I call it leaving all the fun out of living."

Mandie looked up as Morning Star placed a plate of

hot bread in front of them. "Eat," said Morning Star loudly.

"Thank you," Mandie said. "You eat, too." After each of the young people had taken some bread, Mandie handed the plate back to Morning Star.

Joe started to get up. "Let me carry the plate back for you."

Morning Star stepped back. "Sit! I take," she said sternly. Carrying the plate around the table she sat down next to Uncle Ned and helped herself.

Joe looked puzzled. "Did I make her angry?" he asked.

"You are our guest," Sallie told him. "She must serve you. You must not serve her."

"Sorry," Joe apologized. "I forgot she has a different way of doing things."

"Have you been to see this silly school that Mandie goes to, Joe?" Sallie asked, returning to the previous subject.

Joe grinned and swung his feet under the table.

"You bet I've been to that school. I've helped Mandie and her friend, Celia, solve some pretty baffling mysteries around that place," he said.

"Mysteries around the school?" Sallie questioned.

Joe looked at Mandie, waiting for her to explain as he dug into the food heaped on his plate.

"We heard a mysterious noise in the attic when I first went there. We got that solved and then we found a terrible secret in an old trunk in the attic," Mandie explained between bites of food. "It's a terribly long story."

At that moment Mandie's great uncle, Wirt Pindar, from Bird-town, came through the open doorway, followed by his grandson, Tsa'ni. Uncle Ned motioned for them to sit at the table.

"Sit. Eat," Uncle Ned told them.

As they sat down, Morning Star got up, gave them plates, and passed the food.

"Hello, Uncle Wirt, Tsa'ni," Mandie greeted them across the table.

"Glad to see Papoose." Uncle Wirt beamed. "And doctor boy."

"How are you, sir," Joe replied.

Tsa'ni nodded his head at Mandie but did not smile or speak.

As the adults began discussing the hospital, the young people listened.

"Walls torn down every day," Uncle Wirt told them. "Every day work done is torn down."

"And nobody has seen anyone around there?" Uncle John asked.

"Moongo, she come back after many, many years. Married to Catawba man, Running Fire. Two big sons, live near to hospital. See nothing, hear nothing," Uncle Wirt replied.

"Moongo? I remember her from when I was a small boy. She must be old by now," Uncle John said. "So she finally came back. Where do they live, Uncle Wirt? I don't remember any cabin anywhere near the hospital."

"Live in old horse barn near creek," Uncle Wirt explained. "We put man to guard hospital tonight."

"Moongo and her family are that close but don't ever hear anything going on? That's strange," Uncle John mused.

"I haven't even seen the hospital yet," Mandie put in. "How much have they got done?"

"Rock on ground for bottom," Uncle Wirt told her. "Wood for floor. All still there. But when walls made, walls get torn down."

"Uncle John, when are we going to see it?" Mandie asked.

"We'll go early tomorrow morning," Uncle John replied. "I think one of us ought to stay with the guard every night after the workmen leave."

Uncle Ned spoke up. "Dimar say he watch."

"Dimar?" Mandie and Joe said together.

"Dimar say he wait for us at hospital tomorrow," Uncle Wirt answered.

"I'm so glad we're going to get to see Dimar," Mandie remarked.

Joe looked at her with a hint of jealousy in his eyes. "Yes, we will all be glad to see Dimar," he said.

"Remember how you and Dimar caught those thieves who set fire to my grandfather's barn?" Sallie asked Joe.

"Yeh, and I think Dimar and I can catch whoever is tearing down the hospital," Joe replied. "Mr. Shaw, may I have your permission to help Dimar guard the hospital tomorrow night?"

"Well, I suppose so, but your father should be here before tomorrow night. You'll have to ask him, of course," Uncle John said. "You boys will have to promise not to let anyone see you. They could harm you. All we want you to do is watch, and when you see someone doing this malicious work, you hurry and get us men. Is that understood?"

"But I'm almost fourteen," Joe protested. "And so is Dimar. We could put up a pretty good fight."

"No, no, that won't ever do. You might get hurt," Uncle John told him. "The only way I'll let you stay out there is under the conditions I've mentioned."

"Well, all right, sir. I'll do whatever you say," Joe gave in.

Mandie turned to Joe. "You and Dimar will see all the excitement. Sallie and I will miss out on that," she protested.

"You'll find out what's going on when we come back to tell Mr. Shaw that there's someone there," Joe told her.

"*If* you come back," Mandie replied. "I know you."

Tsa'ni sat through the whole conversation without saying a word. He listened and took it all in.

Chapter 4 / The Torn-Down Hospital

The first bright rays of sunshine the next morning peeped through the upstairs window and played around on Mandie's face. Opening her eyes and squinting in the light, Mandie looked around bewildered. Then she saw Sallie sleeping next to her on the cornshuck mattress and she remembered that she was in Uncle Ned's house. Also, her friend Joe was sleeping on the other side of the rough wall dividing the attic into two rooms. And today was the day she was to finally see the hospital being built.

Slipping out of bed, trying not to wake Sallie, she quickly pulled her cotton nightgown over her tousled blonde curls. Snowball jumped down and rubbed around her legs as he meowed. Hastily grabbing the dress hanging on a nail near the bed, she pulled it over her head and buttoned the waist.

Sallie sat up, rubbed her eyes and smiled at her friend. She rolled out of bed.

"You are up early this morning," Sallie said, exchanging her gown for her red flowered skirt and white waist.

"I don't want to waste a minute. We're going to see the hospital, remember?" Mandie told her, quickly brushing her long hair and braiding it into one long plait down her back.

"Hey, wait for me!" Joe called from the other side of the partition.

"I'll meet you downstairs," Mandie yelled back at him, tying her apron over her blue gingham dress.

"I smell coffee," Joe called from the other side.

"My grandmother is already up. She gets up before daylight every morning," Sallie said loudly to Joe. She hurriedly tied her dark hair back with a red ribbon.

The three of them scrambled for the ladder to go downstairs. Joe managed to get down first and stood there waiting for the girls. Mandie had to carry Snowball down. He refused to go down the ladder.

"Aren't y'all pokey this morning?" Joe teased, standing with his long legs spread apart and his hands on his thin hips.

"You won because your legs are longer than ours. It wasn't a fair race," Mandie told him, setting Snowball on the floor and straightening the skirt of her dress.

Joe, laughing, told them, "Come on. Let's see who gets to the washpan first." He turned to run across the room, Sallie and Mandie following. The girls lined up behind Joe to wash their faces and hands.

Morning Star, Uncle Ned, Elizabeth and Uncle John, sitting at the table, looked at them in surprise.

"What's the big hurry?" Uncle John asked.

Mandie's blue eyes sparkled. "We want to go to the hospital."

"But it isn't far from here," said Uncle John. "We don't have to hurry that much."

Elizabeth smiled. "She wants to hurry up and get this thing settled so we can go to Charleston," she explained.

"You are going to Charleston?" Sallie's eyes grew wide.

"Yes, if we can straighten everything out here, we're going to Charleston to see the ocean," Mandie told her.

"You mean you're going to see some boy you met at that school in Asheville," Joe retorted, sitting down at the table.

Elizabeth and John looked at each other with raised eyebrows.

"Joe Woodard, hush up," said Mandie, as she and Sallie sat down next to him. "We're just going to stay at his parents' home."

"Well, that's going to see him, isn't it?" Joe sounded angry.

Elizabeth interrupted. "Yes, Joe, we are going to visit Thomas Patton and his parents. Amanda met Thomas while she was at school. My family has known the Pattons for years. So we're going to visit them, and also give Amanda an opportunity to see the ocean for the first time."

Joe meekly bowed his head. "Yes, ma'am, I understand," he said.

Uncle Ned spoke up, "Thank Big God, John Shaw."

John gave thanks and when he had finished, the old Indian said loudly, "Eat!"

Morning Star ladled out the hot mush.

As they ate and talked, Uncle Wirt and Tsa'ni came in and joined them at the table. Tsa'ni remained silent but listened to every word of the excited conversation.

Before long, everyone except Morning Star piled into Uncle Ned's big wagon and they were on their way. In a short while they rounded a bend in the dirt road. Through the branches of the trees and bushes, Mandie caught her first glimpse of the structure that would be the hospital for the Cherokees.

She was breathless. "Look!" she cried.

Uncle Ned stopped the wagon a little farther down the road, and Mandie jumped down. As she ran around the building, she saw the splintered planks all around that had evidently been part of the walls. Then something caught her eye. Hastening to look behind the building site, she found a man gagged and blindfolded, tied up and lying on the ground. She screamed to the others.

When Uncle Wirt arrived, he stooped to untie the man. "This Kent, man who watch last night."

As the man was released from all the ropes, he took a deep breath and managed to sit up.

Uncle John squatted down beside Kent. "What happened?" he asked.

"I don't rightly know," said the man, trying to wet his parched lips with his tongue. "I was walkin' 'round, lookin', and all of a sudden somethin' hit me hard on the noggin. That's all I 'member. I wakes up, can't see, can't move."

Elizabeth brought water from the barrel that Uncle Ned kept in his wagon. She offered a dipperful to the man. He greedily swallowed it and stood up, stretching his cramped limbs.

"Are you all right?" Uncle John asked. "I'm sorry about this. We'll just have to post another guard with you. They won't be able to surprise two at one time."

"Sorry, mister, but I don't want the job," Kent said. "You see, I'm one of the carpenters tryin' to build this thing. I just wanted to make a little extry money stayin' at night, but it ain't worth it. I'll keep on workin' in the daytime with the others, but no more night work for me."

Uncle Ned pointed to the road. "Men come to work," he said as a group of white men arrived in a wagon loaded with lumber and tools.

The workmen got off the wagon and advanced toward the group. Looking around they shook their heads in disgust when they saw their previous day's work lying in ruins.

"Mornin', Mr. Shaw," said the leader. "Sure glad that you come to do somethin' about this. If that ain't the beatin'est thing I ever heerd of. Fast as we'uns builds it, summins else is atearin' it down."

As the workers stood staring at the mess, Uncle John called to Mandie, and she came to his side. "Amanda, this is Mr. Green," said Uncle John. "He's in charge of building this hospital. Mr. Green, this is my niece, Amanda Shaw, who discovered the Cherokees' gold and is responsible for this hospital being built in the first place," he said proudly.

Mandie stepped forward, holding out her small white hand. "How do you do, Mr. Green," she said, shaking his big rough hand. "I know it's frustrating to you to have your work undone every night, but we are here to do something about it. And I think we can find a way to stop it."

"Yes, ma'am," Mr. Green said, in awe of the well-spoken young girl who had such a great responsibility. He had heard the whole story.

Suddenly Mandie saw Dimar emerge from the bushes. His great admiration for her gleamed in his eyes. Mandie immediately dropped her ladylike air as she raced to meet him.

"Dimar!" she cried, catching his brown hand in hers. "I'm so glad to see you. It's been so long."

"Yes, it has been a long time," Dimar replied, transfixed by her friendly greeting. He withdrew his hand and stepped toward the others. Mandie walked by his side.

"Good morning," he said to the waiting group. "Either you are early or I am late."

"We not here long," said Uncle Ned as Sallie and Joe greeted the boy.

"Dimar, it's a pleasure to see you again," Uncle John told him.

"You just missed the excitement," said Mandie. "Last night someone tied up Kent, over there, and just left him. We found him just a few minutes ago."

"I promise to stay tonight and watch," said Dimar. "I will not let them tie me up."

"I have permission to stay with you, Dimar," Joe told him.

"Between the two of us nothing will happen tonight," Dimar said.

Sallie smiled at Tsa'ni, who was standing nearby. "Tsa'ni, are you staying with Joe and Dimar also?" she asked.

Everyone grew silent, waiting for his reply.

Tsa'ni rubbed the toe of his moccasin in the dirt. "No, I do not wish to stay," he said.

The others pretended they had heard nothing and went on discussing the forthcoming night.

"All right, Mr. Green, we will be back before you quit work at five o'clock," said Uncle John. "And we'll do everything possible to catch these vandals tonight."

"It sho' is disgustin' to do all that hard work and then have somebody tear it all down," Mr. Green replied. "I sho' hope you catch 'em, and I hope the punishment ain't too mild."

"I can assure you it will be quite severe," Uncle John promised.

Uncle Ned examined the splintered boards scattered

all around. "No piece of wall good. Must have new boards," he said, stooping and tossing the wood around.

"We got a load of boards in the wagon, and we got 'nother one comin'," Mr. Green said. "Sho' is a waste of money to buy all them boards and have 'em split up that way."

Mandie was not worried about the money. The supply of gold seemed endless. "It's a waste of time, too," she said. "This hospital needs to be finished so it can be used."

"Used?" Joe queried. "Who's sick?"

"Joe," Mandie said with irritation, "your father will be coming here at least once a month to keep up with everyone's health. Besides, we're going to hire a nurse who will stay here all the time."

"This is a wonderful thing for the Cherokees," Sallie told her.

"Humph!" Tsa'ni grunted.

Dimar frowned at Tsa'ni. "The Cherokees do get sick once in a while, and they need a doctor just like everyone else," he said. "Remember the last time these people visited, when you hurt your foot in that trap and had to have a doctor?"

Tsa'ni silently turned on his heel and walked away toward Uncle Ned's wagon.

"If he need doctor, he be glad hospital here," Uncle Wirt said.

Joe looked longingly at the workmen. "Could I stay here all day and help the men work?" he asked John Shaw.

"I would like to help, too," said Dimar.

Uncle John looked thoughtful for a moment. "No, that's impossible," he said. "You don't have anything with you to eat, and you wouldn't have any way to get back to Uncle Ned's. Let's go back now, and after we have our noon meal, you and Dimar can ride two of the horses back out here. How's that?"

"Thanks, Mr. Shaw," Joe said, smiling.

"Thank you, sir," Dimar added.

"Before we go, Uncle John," Mandie began, "tell me something about the hospital, please."

"What do you want to know, Amanda?" Uncle John asked.

Mandie turned, walked up the steps, and paced the floor of the building. Sallie followed.

"How is it to be arranged?" Mandie asked. "You know, how many beds will it hold and how many rooms, and all that?"

Uncle John joined them. "You see all those posts standing up around here?" he said. "They are called studs. They will be covered with boards to make the interior walls and divide the hospital into rooms. The studs will be four feet apart around each room, and then you have to allow four feet for the doors. So if you'll just walk around and look at the studs you can figure out how many rooms there will be and how big each one will be."

The two girls walked about and counted the posts.

"Here's one big room," Mandie said, pointing to one section. "There's another smaller room, and another, and another, and then here's a long narrow room, too narrow for beds, I think. What is this room for?"

"That is the office," he told her. "The records will be kept there. Dr. Woodard will use it, and when you come to visit, Amanda, that will be your office."

"Me? An office? What for, Uncle John?" Mandie asked in surprise.

"You told your mother and me that you would like to know what's going on with the money since you are responsible for it, so we thought we'd just make you a little office right here," he teased.

"Oh, I don't need an office. I depend on you to keep up with things, especially while I'm away at school," Mandie told him. "That will have to be your office and Dr. Woodard's."

"Anyway, we need an office for records," he told her.

Mandie looked across the other side of the building. "That big room looks like it would hold about ten single beds," she calculated. "How many windows will it have?"

"One on each end and two on the side, I believe," Uncle John replied. "Why? Are you planning on making the curtains for it?"

"That's a good idea!" Mandie exclaimed. "Sallie, could you make some of them and I'll make some?"

Elizabeth called to her, "Amanda, don't forget you'll be away at school. You won't have time to make curtains."

"I suppose not," she decided. "I'll just have to get Aunt Lou to make them. She can make anything, Sallie. You'll have to come to visit us in Franklin again."

"I hope to someday," Sallie assured her. "I would like to get up there."

"Oh, yes, you've got to," Mandie agreed.

"Right now, girls, I think we'd better see Morning Star. She probably has a good hot meal waiting," Uncle John reminded them.

"Yeh, let's hurry so Dimar and I can come back and do some work," Joe put in.

When they returned to Uncle Ned's house, Morning Star had the table set and food waiting. Dr. Woodard was just pulling up in his buggy, and Joe ran out to take the horse for him.

"Mr. Shaw is having the hospital guarded at night, Dad," Joe informed his father. "Dimar has volunteered to stay all night, and Mr. Shaw said I could, too, with your permission." He held up his hand. "Before you protest, we aren't going to let anyone see us," he said, helping unhitch the horse and buggy. "If someone comes around, we're going to hightail it back to Uncle Ned's and get the men. Is it all right if I stay? Please, Dad?"

"I suppose so, provided you don't try to defend the place. Leave that to the men," Dr. Woodard told him. "If you see anyone around, you get out of there. People of that nature could be dangerous."

"Thanks, Dad," Joe said. "I promise."

After hurrying through dinner, Joe and Dimar asked to be excused, then ran to the barn to saddle two horses.

Mandie and Sallie waved good-bye to them.

"Joe, please catch those crooks tonight, but be careful. You, too, Dimar," Mandie called to the boys.

"Yes, please be careful," Sallie added.

"We know your Uncle John's orders," Joe called to them. "If we see or hear anything, we are not to let them see us, and we are to come back immediately for help."

"That's right, boys," Uncle John told them.

Tsa'ni stood by, watching and saying nothing.

"So they are off," Sallie said as the boys disappeared in a cloud of dust down the road.

She and Mandie sat down on an old log.

"I think that we should ask God to watch over them," said Mandie, her brow furrowed with concern.

"I agree," Sallie replied.

Taking the Indian girl's dark hand in her white one,

Mandie looked toward the sky. "Dear God," she said, "please take care of Joe and Dimar and keep them from harm. And please help us catch those crooks. Thank you, dear God. Amen."

"Amen," Sallie echoed.

The girls didn't realize then how badly Joe and Dimar would need help.

Chapter 5 / Joe Disappears

Mandie and Sallie spent the afternoon under a huge chestnut tree in Uncle Ned's yard talking about Mandie's school, its strange rules, and its strict headmistresses, Miss Prudence and Miss Hope. The Indian girl was fascinated with Mandie's stories about her friend Celia Hamilton, and the school troublemaker, April Snow.

"Your grandfather, Uncle Ned, comes to visit me at the school, you know," Mandie told her.

"Yes, I know that. He promised your father he would watch over you, so he keeps his promise. But he never tells me anything about your school. He just says you are all right and you send your love, and all that."

"He has never been inside the school," Mandie explained. "When he comes to see me, he always waits for me under the magnolia trees after the ten o'clock bell has rung at night. By then everyone is supposed to be in bed."

"Why are you not also in bed then?" Sallie asked.

"Because I've always been afraid to ask permission to see him. You see, Miss Prudence would probably forbid it," Mandie replied.

"Why? Why would she forbid you to see my grand-father?"

Mandie looked at her friend, trying to soften her ex-planation. "Sallie, you haven't been out into the big world, like at the school," Mandie began. "You see, some white people just don't like Indians. I didn't know that either until my father died and I had to leave Charley Gap."

"You mean they don't like some people just because they are a different color, a different kind of people?" Sallie asked, puzzled.

"You know how Tsa'ni is always making remarks against the white people? That's the way some white people are about Indians," Mandie explained. "Even though God made us all, some white people would have you think Indians were just ... just ... trash or something."

"Do these white people know you are one-fourth Cherokee?" the Indian girl asked.

"They know. There was a big ruckus one day when April Snow spread the word that I was part Indian. But Miss Prudence put a stop to that real fast," Mandie said.

Sallie looked confused. "But you said these people at the school do not like Indians."

"Even though I'm part Indian, Miss Prudence wouldn't dare treat me differently. You see, my Grandmother Taft is a terror sometimes." She laughed. "She has a lot of influence among the rich people who send their daugh-ters to the school. Miss Prudence wouldn't want to get on the wrong side of my grandmother."

"I agree that this is a very silly school you are in," said Sallie. "They do not seem to be honest. They let wealth decide who to be nice to."

"You're exactly right, Sallie," Mandie replied. "I wish I

could live with my Cherokee kinpeople. There is such a difference."

"Maybe someday you can," Sallie said. "But your mother wants you to be educated at that school, so you must do what she says."

"Yes, I know," Mandie replied. "I miss my father so much. If he had lived longer, maybe he and my mother would have got back together again."

"But your father was married to that other woman," Sallie reminded her.

"I know, but things could have been different if my mother had known about me, that I didn't really die when I was born, and that her mother, my Grandmother Taft, told my father that my mother didn't love him anymore."

"Your grandmother told your mother that you died when you were born and made your father take you away so your mother would not try to find your father or you. Your grandmother thought she was doing the best thing for everyone," Sallie said.

"I suppose she did," Mandie said with a big sigh.

"Do you dislike your grandmother because she separated your mother and your father and you?" Sallie asked.

"No, I don't dislike her. In fact, she's my friend. At first she wouldn't have anything to do with me. But then after my mother married Uncle John, and I came to school in Asheville where she lives, I finally got to know her."

"Does Joe let you know what is going on at Charley Gap since you left there?"

"As much as he can find out," Mandie replied. Looking into her friend's dark eyes she added, "Joe promised to get my father's house back for me when he gets old enough."

"And how is he going to do that?" Sallie asked.

Mandie laughed. "I'm not sure. He just said leave it to him. Joe wants to be a lawyer, you know."

"Then he will learn how to get the house back," Sallie assured her. "Joe is a brave boy."

Mandie looked at her in surprise. "You think so?"

"Yes, look what he is doing right now. He is risking his life to save the hospital for you," Sallie replied.

"I know it's dangerous," said Mandie, "but we have asked God to take care of them. We must trust God."

Meanwhile Joe and Dimar were working hard with the men, replacing wall boards at the hospital. When the workmen left for the day at five o'clock, all the walls were up around the structure.

Joe and Dimar washed their faces and hands in the nearby creek, then sat down on the hospital steps to eat their supper.

Uncovering the basket Morning Star had packed, Joe examined its contents. "Can you tell what this is?" he asked. "Is it fried chicken, rabbit, or what?"

Dimar laughed. "Now you know that is fried chicken," he said. "Can you not smell it?"

Joe spread the cloth on the steps and laid out the food. "I guess so, but I just plain don't like some of those other things that Morning Star cooks up. I'm not used to it," Joe told him.

"Like we Cherokees are not used to some things that the white people eat." Dimar laughed. "But I think we both like fried chicken, and Morning Star knows that."

"Do you think she notices when there are some things I don't eat at her house?" Joe asked, alarmed.

"Yes, she notices and she understands. So she tries to please you," Dimar explained.

"Goodness. I guess I'm a lot of trouble then," Joe said.

"No more than anyone else," Dimar assured him.

Joe hungrily ate the chicken with his fingers, cramming in a bite of biscuit now and then, and drinking a little coffee to wash it all down.

"I suppose one of us ought to stay at the front of the building and the other one at the back. That way it would be easier to see anyone who comes up," Joe suggested.

"Yes, I will stay at the back, and you stay here at the front," Dimar agreed. "But we must stay far enough back in the bushes so no one will see us."

Joe looked concerned. "I hope they don't see the horses."

"I do not think they will if the horses will just be contented to stay quietly down by the creek," the Indian boy said. "If one of us sees someone coming here to do damage, we must let the other one know. Then one of us will ride quickly to get Mr. Shaw and the others."

So it was agreed. The two boys walked quietly back and forth in the bushes, keeping an eye on the building. Now and then they would meet each other and turn back. They talked very little and then only in low whispers.

It grew dark. The birds settled down for the night. Frogs began croaking along the creek. Here and there lightning bugs flashed their lights. The scent of clean creek water drifted into the air. The horses seemed to be well satisfied as they continued to graze in the darkness. The two boys grew bored and weary.

Joe stopped Dimar as they met in the bushes on one of their patrols. "How about some of that sweetcake and coffee that we've got left?" he whispered softly.

"That sounds good," said Dimar.

"I'll get it," Joe volunteered. Groping his way through the bushes to the basket they had hung on a tree limb near the horses, he took it down and hurried back uphill.

Sitting down by Dimar, who sat waiting in the woods, Joe uncovered the basket.

"It's so dark, I can't see too well," Joe told him. "But take what you want and then I'll get mine." He held out the basket.

"Here is a piece of the cake," said Dimar, feeling around in the dark basket. "And I think this is the jar of coffee I was drinking out of before."

"And I'll have the same," Joe said, reaching inside. He took a big bite of cake. "Mmm, this is good," he said.

"It will help us stay awake and alert," the Indian boy said.

"I can—" Joe began to speak and then stopped, motioning Dimar to silence. "Listen," he whispered.

Someone was walking through the brush. The boys dropped their cake back into the basket and rose to their feet. The footsteps came closer.

"There is more than one person," Dimar whispered in Joe's ear.

Then there was a loud bang as something crashed against the wooden walls of the hospital.

"Quick! You go for the men! You ride faster than I do," Joe told Dimar in a low whisper. "I'll stay here and watch."

"Do not let them see you," Dimar warned as he ran for one of the horses nearby.

Joe stood frozen to the spot. Dimar was so quiet that Joe didn't hear him lead the horse away before mounting. Joe's heartbeat quickened in anger at the thought of someone tearing down the walls. He edged closer to the structure. He could hear talking, but it was too low to be understood. As he moved still closer, he could see three men with axes standing by the hospital. In the darkness he could not tell whether they were Indians or white men. He moved just a little closer. A dry twig cracked loudly under his foot.

The three men turned in his direction and listened. Then they moved forward quietly to investigate.

Joe stood motionless, hoping they wouldn't hear him breathing. Suddenly the three men came at him.

As Joe tried to flee, the men spread out and surrounded him. In the scuffle, they caught him by his shirt and tore it off him. Then they pulled Joe closer for a better look.

"Nobody we know," one man said. The other two agreed.

Quickly the men pulled out rope and handkerchiefs from their pockets. Even though Joe put up a good fight, they managed to gag and bind him.

After carrying Joe away from the hospital, the three men picked up their axes and completely wrecked the walls. Satisfied with their destruction, they pulled Joe to his feet and pushed him ahead as they tromped off into the woods.

As Dimar arrived back at Uncle Ned's house, he called to the men for help. Within minutes Uncle Ned, Uncle John, Uncle Wirt, and Dr. Woodard had dressed and saddled horses to return with the boy to the hospital. Tsa'ni had already gone home.

When the girls heard the commotion, they hurriedly dressed enough to get downstairs before the men left. Elizabeth and Morning Star were there, too.

"Dimar, is Joe all right?" Mandie asked anxiously. "You

left him alone with those crooks."

"He is all right, Mandie. He is not with the crooks. I left him hidden in the bushes," the Indian boy told her.

"Please hurry, Dimar," Sallie urged him. "And be careful."

"I will," the boy promised. Hurrying outside, he rode quietly off into the night with the men.

"Amanda, Sallie, if you're staying up, we might as well have some tea," Elizabeth told the girls. "Morning Star is getting it ready."

"I couldn't go to bed with all this going on," Mandie told her mother.

Mandie and Sallie pulled chairs over in front of the huge fireplace. Morning Star poked at the fire and soon had a nice blaze going.

Mandie shivered. "I'm so excited, I'm cold."

"So am I," Sallie admitted.

"I know it gets cold in these mountains at night, but it's partly nerves, too," Elizabeth told them. "The tea will help."

Sallie looked around the room. "Mandie, where is Snowball?" she asked.

Mandie jumped up to look for him. Then she laughed as she saw the white kitten perched at the top of the attic ladder. He looked down at them, whining. Climbing the ladder, Mandie picked up her kitten and brought him down.

"Snowball, you've got to learn to come down the ladder, you silly cat," she said.

When she set him down in front of the fire, he curled up and began purring while the women and girls drank hot tea and discussed the chances of catching the crooks.

Before the men got very close to the hospital, they dismounted to avoid being heard.

"Must be quiet," Uncle Ned told the others as he led the way on foot.

Silently, they crept through the bushes. As they came within sight of the hospital, the clouds uncovered the moon. The men stopped in horror when they saw the destruction. Circling around, they found no one.

"They're gone," Uncle John said.

Dr. Woodard looked around for his son. "Where is Joe, Dimar?"

"We were in the bushes down this way," Dimar said, leading them into the woods. "Joe," he called out, "it is Dimar. Joe, where are you?"

There wasn't a sound except for the restless horse that Joe had left down by the creek.

"Did you remind him not to let anyone see him?" Uncle John asked.

"Yes, sir," Dimar replied. "He said he would stay out of sight."

As Uncle Ned scoured the bushes, he found Joe's torn shirt.

"Here, boy shirt," Uncle Ned said, holding it up for everyone to see. "Torn."

Dr. Woodard stepped forward and took the shirt. "Looks like he might have been in a fight," he said.

"I sure hope the boy is all right," Uncle John said.

"We find. We follow feet marks," Uncle Wirt assured him, bending to search the ground.

Then the moon went back under the clouds, and it was too dark to find anything.

"It shouldn't be too long till daylight," Uncle John said. "We'll just have to stay here and wait until we can see."

Dr. Woodard sat down on the hospital steps. "We're in a bigger mess now than ever," he said. "The crooks not only got away with their vandalism, but they've evidently kidnapped my boy."

"I am sorry, sir," Dimar said.

"I'm not blaming anyone but Joe," Dr. Woodard replied. "He's headstrong sometimes, and he probably got excited and let them see him."

"We find doctor boy, and we find crooks," Uncle Ned told him.

"We find," Uncle Wirt echoed.

"Yes," said Uncle John. "And this destruction is disgusting. We've got to put a stop to it somehow."

At the first crack of dawn the search began. The old Indians were able to pick up a trail, but it seemed to circle around and then disappear into the creek. They spread out and combed every inch of the surrounding bushes without success.

When the sun came up, the workmen came to the hospital site and looked around angrily.

"Done it agin, heh? We's expectin' it," Mr. Green called to Uncle John. " 'Bout par for the course."

"That's not all they did this time," Uncle John told him. "They've evidently kidnapped one of the boys who stood guard last night."

The other workmen gathered around.

Mr. Green whistled. "You don't say! What are you goin' to do?"

"Since you are here, I think we might as well go home, eat a bite, and break the news to the women. Then we'll come back for an all-day search," said Uncle John.

The others agreed, and within minutes they had

mounted their horses and were heading back to Uncle Ned's house.

When Mandie and Sallie heard them coming, they ran to the door. Mandie looked around quickly. "Where's Joe?" she asked.

Uncle John came into the room, put his arm around her shoulders, and led her over to the warmth of the fireplace. "I'm afraid we don't know where Joe is right now," he said. "He seems to have disappeared."

"Disappeared? Oh, Uncle John, where is he?" Mandie demanded, her eyes filling with tears. "Where is he?"

Dr. Woodard walked over to Mandie and took her hand. "We'll find him, Amanda," he assured her. "You know Joe. He likes to go off and do things on his own. He—"

"Dr. Woodard!" Mandie interrupted, spying Joe's shirt under the doctor's arm. She snatched it from him and sank into a chair in shock. "Oh, please, dear God," Mandie cried, "don't let anything happen to Joe! Please send him back to us. Please, dear God!"

Tears filled every eye in the room.

Chapter 6 / The Search

Dimar and the men hurriedly ate a good hot meal, but no one said much. They were all worried about Joe. Mandie couldn't speak a word without breaking into tears, and Sallie stayed right by her side. Dimar kept blaming himself. Although Dr. Woodard tried to keep his emotions under control, it was obvious that he, too, was very worried.

Just as the men were about to leave, Tsa'ni appeared in the doorway.

Uncle Wirt frowned at his grandson. "Where you been?" he asked roughly.

"I have been home. I came to help you search for Joe," Tsa'ni replied, his gaze never wavering from his grandfather's angry, wrinkled face.

"Joe?" Mandie spoke up. "How did you know about Joe?"

Everyone stared at Tsa'ni. No one outside their own group knew about Joe's disappearance.

Uncle Wirt grabbed Tsa'ni by the shoulder. "How you know? How?" the old man demanded.

Tsa'ni dropped his eyes and stuttered, "Why . . . I . . .

I . . . I came by the hospital. The men working there told me."

"I don't believe you, Tsa'ni," Mandie said. "I don't believe you at all."

"What you do at hospital?" Uncle Wirt asked, still holding the boy's shoulder.

"I . . . I . . ." Tsa'ni stammered again, looking at the floor.

"Why *did* you come by the hospital?" Mandie interrupted, moving closer. "You wouldn't even volunteer to stand guard with Dimar and Joe last night."

Uncle John put his arm around Mandie's shoulder. "Amanda, please—" he said, trying to calm her. Mandie didn't want to be calmed. "Tsa'ni, I suppose you already know who the crooks are. That's why you didn't want to help out last night."

Tsa'ni stared at her. "They are not crooks who tear down the hospital," he said firmly. "They are the spirits of the Cherokee. They do not believe in the white man's medicine."

"Spirits of the Cherokee?" Mandie echoed.

"No such thing," grunted Uncle Wirt, angrily.

Uncle Ned stepped forward. "The spirits of our Cherokee do not do bad things," he said. "Tsa'ni, *you* bad Cherokee."

Morning Star stood near the fireplace, obviously confused about what was happening. Uncle Ned turned to her and explained rapidly in Cherokee. The old woman suddenly grabbed the homemade broom from the hearth and ran toward Tsa'ni, screaming in Cherokee.

Uncle Wirt let go of Tsa'ni's shoulder and pushed him toward the angry woman waving the broom.

Tsa'ni jumped backward toward the door. "Just wait.

You will see!" he yelled at Mandie as he turned and quickly ran out the doorway.

Mandie walked over to Uncle Ned. "What does Tsa'ni mean?" she asked, looking up into the old man's face. "What is he talking about?"

Uncle Ned took her small white hand in his old, wrinkled one. "Papoose, not worry," he said. "Tsa'ni bad Cherokee. Speak wash hog."

Mandie looked at him questioningly. Then a little smile played on her face. "You mean *hogwash*, Uncle Ned."

Uncle Ned smiled too. "Story hogwash," he said. "Do not believe."

"I don't believe him. But where in the world did he get such an idea?" Mandie asked.

The old Indian touched his forehead with his finger. "Here," he said. "Tsa'ni have crazy thoughts here. Papoose not listen to him. We find Joe. We find crooks."

Mandie turned to her mother and Uncle. "I'm going with you, Uncle John," she declared.

"No, Amanda," Elizabeth told her. "You must stay here with Morning Star and Sallie. The men can do a better job without us. Besides, you didn't get much sleep last night, waiting for them to come back."

"But, Mother, that's Joe we're looking for. If it was me lost somewhere, Joe would be right along in the search. I have to go, Mother. Please?" Mandie begged.

"I said no, Amanda," Elizabeth replied firmly.

"Mother, please let me go," Mandie tried again. Then, turning to Uncle John and looking at him with tear-filled blue eyes, she asked, "Please, Uncle John, may I go?"

"Amanda," Elizabeth said sharply.

"Well," Uncle John hesitated. He could never refuse

those blue eyes anything. "Elizabeth, I think she'd be all right with us."

"Please, Mother?" Mandie pleaded. "I couldn't bear to sit here and wait all that time. Please let me go."

"Well, Elizabeth?" Uncle John waited for a reply.

"Oh, John, you two always win out," Elizabeth said, giving up. "But, Amanda, you must promise me to be careful and to stay with the men at all times. No wandering off alone."

"Yes, ma'am. I promise." Mandie moved to her mother's side and squeezed her hand. "Thank you, Mother."

Sallie looked at her grandfather. "May I go, too?" she asked.

Uncle Ned grunted and then spoke to Morning Star in Cherokee.

The old squaw smiled at Sallie and rattled off something in their native language.

Sallie's eyes sparkled as she answered in Cherokee, then turned to Mandie, who waited breathlessly for the verdict. "My grandmother says I may go, too. But I also have to stay near the men."

"I'm glad, Sallie. I was afraid to ask if you could go, too," Mandie said.

Dr. Woodard stood up from the table. "Well, if y'all are ready, I say let's hit the road."

Uncle John nodded. "Yes, I think we're all ready now." He turned to kiss Elizabeth. "Pray for us, dear."

"I will," Elizabeth promised. "And Dr. Woodard, my heart goes out to you. I hope you come back with Joe."

"Thank you, dear," the doctor replied, patting Elizabeth's shoulder. "I sure hope so too."

They all went outside where the horses were saddled and waiting.

"Must get more horses for Papooses," Uncle Ned said, walking toward the fenced pasture where the animals grazed.

Dimar followed him. "I will help," he said.

When they brought out two ponies for the girls, everyone mounted and waved good-bye to Morning Star and Elizabeth. Mandie balanced Snowball on her shoulder, and they galloped off down the road.

The search was tiresome. They left the horses at the creek in the woods by the hospital, hoping to return before the workmen left for the day. Then they invaded the bushes, searching and calling Joe's name.

As they walked along the creek bank, it became an uphill climb, and Mandie looked around, sensing something familiar. "Sallie, isn't this the way to the cave?" she asked her friend.

"Yes, it is," Sallie replied.

Mandie spoke to Uncle Ned, just ahead of them. "Are we going to the cave where we found the gold, Uncle Ned?"

The old man turned around. "Cave fell in, remember? All closed up now. Rockslide," he said. "We pass it soon, Papoose. We look in mountain for doctor boy."

"And we will stop by my house to rest and eat," Dimar spoke up from behind Mandie. "My mother will have food ready."

"It will be nice to see your mother again," Mandie told him.

The group tramped on through the bushes, climbing the steep mountainside. Soon they came within sight of the waterfalls that had hidden the doorway to the old cave.

Mandie stopped and stared. "Look!" she exclaimed.

"The waterfalls have changed, haven't they? Aren't they a little lopsided?" Snowball jumped down from her shoulder.

Everyone stopped to look.

"Rocks slide down, make different shape when cave fell in," Uncle Wirt said.

Dr. Woodard stood by Mandie and put his hand gently on her shoulder. "So that's the cave where you, and Sallie, and Joe found the gold," he said to her. "You know I've never been up through these mountains before."

"Yes, this is it," said Mandie. "I thought everyone knew about this place. You see, you had to walk under the waterfalls to get to the opening in the rock. When you went through that opening, there was a huge dark cave, lots of rooms, and also lots of bats. We frightened them one time, and they went wild, flying all around us."

"And the gold we found was in one of those dark rooms," Sallie added.

"As soon as Uncle Ned and Uncle Wirt took the gold out, the whole cave fell in," Mandie explained. "Rocks came sliding down every which way."

"Joe told me about that," Dr. Woodard said, still staring at the waterfalls. He cleared his throat and moved forward. "Guess we'd better keep on going, so we can find him before dark."

"Yes, we'll have to hurry to cover all this area and get back out before dark catches us," said Uncle John.

The old Indians kept alert as they led the search party. There was no clue or any sign of a trail. Snowball followed Mandie until he became tired and meowed for her to let him ride on her shoulder again.

Finally they came to Dimar's house, a neat log cabin set deep in the woods by a small stream. When the young people spotted the cabin, they hurried ahead, and arrived at the door before the others.

Jerusha Walkingstick, Dimar's mother, stood in the doorway, waiting for them. She embraced the two girls.

"Come! Eat!" she told them, leading the way back into the cabin. Then returning to the door, she beckoned the others.

After they had all gathered around a long table full of food, Uncle Wirt thanked God for their lunch and asked help for finding Joe.

As they ate, Snowball wandered out the open door into the yard. A few moments later there was a loud shot, and a bullet hit a tree near the front door. The kitten came bouncing back into the cabin, his fur ruffled.

The men jumped up, grabbed their rifles, and ran outside. The girls followed. But since there was no one in sight, the men split up, heading different directions toward the surrounding woods.

"You girls stay there with Jerusha," Uncle John called back. "Dimar, you keep watch with them. Back in the house at once, all of you."

The girls obeyed, and Dimar stationed himself at the doorway with his rifle. Standing by the window with Jerusha, Mandie and Sallie watched the men vanish into the woods.

"Dimar, does anyone else live around here?" Mandie asked.

Dimar didn't take his eyes off the yard outside. "No one who would shoot at us," he replied. "There are only friends."

Sallie spoke up. "Then maybe it is someone who does not live in the woods."

"But why would anyone shoot at Dimar's house?" asked Mandie.

"I do not know, but we will find out," Dimar assured her.

After a while the men returned. They stopped to study the tree the bullet hit and then came inside the house.

"There is no one out there," Uncle John said, standing his rifle by the chair where he sat.

Uncle Wirt and Uncle Ned warmed themselves by the fireplace while Dr. Woodard sat back down at the table.

"Did you see anything?" Mandie asked.

"Nothing, Amanda," Dr. Woodard replied.

"But there was a gunshot. I saw the bullet strike the tree," Sallie insisted.

"Yes, there was a gunshot, Sallie, but whoever was shooting got away before we could catch them," said Uncle John.

"We find feet marks. Go in creek," Uncle Ned muttered.

"And we catch," Uncle Wirt added.

Uncle John stood. "If everyone is finished eating, I think we'd better get on our way."

Everyone stood and got ready to leave.

"Thank you, Mrs. Walkingstick, for the food and everything," Dr. Woodard told the woman.

"Yes, we appreciate it, Jerusha," Uncle John said as the two Indian men echoed their thanks.

Jerusha smiled. "Always welcome," she said.

Mandie and Sallie put their arms around the Indian woman. "Thank you," they said in unison.

Jerusha squeezed them tight.

The men started out the doorway, and the girls hurried to catch up.

"Must be careful," Jerusha called after them from the doorway.

"We will," the girls called back. They waved and went on their way.

Again they walked and they walked, through bushes, briars, weeds and swinging tree limbs, but they could find no trail or clue. They met no one and heard nothing.

Although Mandie was soon exhausted, she did not complain. After the fright of the gunshot, Snowball clung to Mandie's shoulder content to be carried along.

Walking through an open meadow between Dimar and Sallie, Mandie turned to the Indian boy and said, "Dimar, you said Joe was all right when you left him at the hospital after the men came. If he promised to stay out of sight, how could he have gotten into trouble?"

"Perhaps the crooks came through the bushes and found him," Sallie suggested.

"Perhaps," Dimar agreed. "But I think whoever shot at the tree by my house is one of the crooks who tore down the walls of the hospital."

"You do? Why?" Mandie asked quickly.

"Because whoever it was, went into the creek so we could not follow his footprints," Dimar observed. "The crooks at the hospital also went into the creek so we could not follow their footprints."

"You are absolutely right," Mandie agreed.

Sallie looked puzzled. "But why would the crooks follow us all the way to your house?"

"I do not know but I intend finding out," said Dimar.

After hours of walking, the tired band of searchers finally got back to the hospital. It was late. The workmen had already left for the day. And again their entire day's work had been torn down.

Gasping in anger, Mandie ran ahead. Then she spied a large piece of cardboard nailed to a post that was left standing. "Look!" she cried, pointing. Hurrying closer, she read out loud, "White man, go home!"

Everyone crowded around.

Uncle Ned grunted loudly. "Crooks are Indians. We stop. Call powwow at council house."

"That is a good idea," said Uncle John.

Uncle Wirt looked very angry. "We tell all Cherokee help find doctor boy. Stop tearing down walls," he said loudly.

They made their plans to call all the Cherokees in the Eastern Nation to the council house the next day.

Chapter 7 / Cherokee Powwow

After mounting up with the others, Mandie sadly turned her pony back onto the trail to Uncle Ned's house. They still had not found Joe, not even a trace of him.

Mandie was worried. Joe could be in danger somewhere, and there was no way for her to help. They had traveled miles and miles that day to no avail. He had to be somewhere. And those crooks had to be somewhere, too. Why couldn't they find Joe or the crooks? *Please, dear God,* she prayed silently as her pony clopped down the trail with the others. *Let them be found. Please let Joe be all right.*

Elizabeth and Morning Star waited for them at the doorway of Uncle Ned's cabin when they returned. The two women silently looked among the group, and when they didn't see Joe, they said nothing.

Mandie jumped down from her pony and ran to her mother's arms. Elizabeth hugged Mandie tightly, smoothing her daughter's tangled blonde hair. Tears flooded Mandie's worried blue eyes. She couldn't control the sobs.

"Darling," her mother whispered, looking over Mandie's head at John.

John shook his head sadly.

Dr. Woodard came over to Mandie and took her in his arms. "Look now, Amanda dear, we've not given up hope yet," he said. "Remember, where there's a will there's a way. So we've got to keep that will in order to find a way."

Mandie looked up at his worried face. "I'm sorry, Dr. Woodard," she sobbed. "I know you are worried about Joe, your own son, but you're trying not to show it."

"We have to trust in the Lord to help us. We can't just give up, Amanda," Dr. Woodard said. "You're worn out. That was quite a trip for a young girl. Why don't you get prettied up a bit, eat some good hot food, and get some rest?"

"I'll try, Dr. Woodard," Mandie said.

"You'd better try real hard, young lady. That's doctor's orders," he said, trying to smile.

Sallie, standing nearby, came to her friend's side. "Come on, Mandie. Let's get washed so we can eat."

Mandie followed her to the washpan at the other end of the big room. After everyone had washed and gathered around the table for prayer, Elizabeth and Morning Star silently dished up hot food.

No one seemed to want to talk about the day's fruitless search. Uncle Ned finally broke the silence. "We send word. All Cherokees powwow in council house when sun comes up tomorrow," he said.

"I will spread the word," Dimar volunteered.

"And I find young braves to help," Uncle Wirt added.

"All Cherokees, every one, must come to council house," Uncle Ned emphasized.

Dr. Woodard looked surprised. "Is it possible to gather all the Cherokees in such short time?" he asked.

"Oh, yes, it has been done before," Uncle John told him. "One Cherokee tells another, and the next one tells another, on down the line. It works pretty good."

"Is there any way I can help, Uncle Ned?" Mandie asked.

Uncle Ned shook his head. "Papoose must stay here. Only braves do this job."

"May I go to the council house for the meeting?" Mandie asked.

"Yes. Papoose Cherokee, too. Must go to powwow," Uncle Ned replied.

Mandie smiled. "Thank you, Uncle Ned."

"I guess I'm the only outsider," Elizabeth remarked.

"Mother of papoose go, watch but not talk or vote," said Uncle Ned.

"I appreciate that," Elizabeth answered.

"Oh, but you forgot. I am also an outsider," Dr. Woodard spoke up.

Uncle Ned said, "Doctor must go, too. Doctor father of lost boy."

"So we will all go to the meeting," Uncle John declared.

After hurriedly finishing their meal, Uncle Wirt and Dimar left to relay the message to all the Cherokees. Mandie and Sallie, exhausted from all the walking, climbed up to the attic room with Snowball and crawled into bed.

Mandie was so worn out that in spite of her worry she soon fell asleep.

The next morning after breakfast, Uncle Wirt and Dimar arrived to ride with the others to the big Cherokee powwow.

In the excitement of getting ready to leave, Uncle John took charge. "You young people ride in the wagon with

Uncle Ned," he said. "The rest of us will go with Uncle Wirt."

Outside, Dimar helped Morning Star onto the seat of Uncle Ned's wagon, and then crawled into the back. Uncle Ned took his place next to Morning Star, and the others got into Uncle Wirt's wagon.

As they rode down the dirt road, Mandie smiled at Dimar. "I hope you had time to get some sleep last night."

"I did," Dimar replied. His dark eyes reflected his admiration for her. "It did not take long to get the message line going."

"Do you think Tsa'ni will be there?" Sallie asked.

"He had better be. This is a meeting for all Cherokees," Dimar said.

"Dimar, do you think all the Cherokees will help look for Joe?" Mandie asked.

"They will be glad to help. Some of them know Joe, and they know he is your friend," Dimar replied as the wagon bounced on down the road.

"But where will they look? We covered so much territory yesterday. I don't see how there could be anywhere else to look," Mandie said.

"They will go over the same area again, and they will also search everyone's house," Dimar answered.

Mandie frowned. "Search everyone's house? Don't they trust each other?"

"Yes, but since it was an Indian who put that note on the hospital wall, there has to be a bad Indian somewhere, and they will not stop until they find the traitor," Dimar explained.

"What will they do when they catch him?" Mandie asked.

"He will be brought before a council meeting," said

Dimar. "The council will decide the punishment. It will be severe, too, for kidnapping someone and damaging Cherokee property," the boy told her.

Sallie spoke up. "I have never heard of a Cherokee doing such a bad thing. They all know the Cherokee laws."

"I hate to see anyone punished, but in this case I think it is right. The crook should have to pay for his bad deeds," Mandie said.

As the young people talked on, the sun climbed higher in the sky and birds sang cheery greetings along the way. Now and then stray pigs ran along the road with chickens, cackling and flying out of their way.

Soon the seven-sided, dome-roofed council house came into view. Hundreds of Cherokees were already milling about, laughing and talking with each other. Most of the women had red kerchiefs tied around their heads. The young girls, dressed in their finest, shyly chatted with the young Indian men. There was a festival air about the meeting.

Uncle Ned pulled into a vacant spot along the road and unhitched the horses. Uncle Wirt stopped his wagon right behind them.

As they all walked to the council house, Elizabeth spoke to Uncle Ned. "Am I supposed to wait outside?" she asked.

"No, sit in backside. Wait there," he said.

"Thank you," Elizabeth replied.

The Indians standing around the entrance smiled at Mandie, then moved aside as Uncle Ned led the way into the building.

Mandie looked around. She had been here once before, but the place still interested her. There were wooden benches to sit on. Huge log poles held up the dome-shaped thatched roof. The symbols of the various clans adorned the posts. The place of the sacred fire was directly ahead as they entered. The six leaders of the clans sat behind the fire.

Uncle Ned motioned for everyone to sit near the front, and then he went to stand behind the fire with the leaders. As he did, all the Cherokees quickly took their seats and became silent.

Mandie sat between Dimar and Sallie. She turned slightly to look behind her. The council house was full. She saw Tsa'ni come down the aisle with two other boys and sit down nearby. Tsa'ni looked directly at Mandie but did not speak.

One of the men behind the fire stood and began waving his arms and chanting loudly in the Cherokee language. Mandie looked at Dimar questioningly.

"He is praying," Dimar whispered.

Mandie smiled and watched as the man sat down. Then Uncle Ned began his speech in Cherokee. His voice was angry and demanding, but Mandie could not understand a thing he was saying.

Dimar leaned toward her and whispered, "He is telling the Cherokees what a disgrace it is that an Indian would kidnap a white boy who is our guest. He also says it is a bad crime to destroy the hospital—Cherokee property."

Sallie helped with the translation, too. "He is telling the Cherokees that every man, woman, and child must stop whatever he is doing and join the search," she whispered. "Nothing else is to be done until Joe is found."

Mandie silently looked around the council house. The Cherokees were listening to every word and nodding in agreement.

Uncle Ned concluded his speech with some loud, angry words. The Cherokees rose to their feet and echoed whatever he had said. As they sat back down, Uncle Ned beckoned to Mandie to come forward.

Her heart beat rapidly. Must she go up there before all these people? She had done it once before but she was so frightened, she could hardly speak. She hesitated but Uncle Ned called loudly, "Come, Papoose."

Sallie and Dimar pulled her to her feet and pushed her out into the aisle.

"But what does he want with me?" she whispered.

"He wants you to speak to your people," Sallie replied.

"Go. He is waiting," Dimar urged.

Uncle Ned stepped down from the platform to meet Mandie on the way. Taking her small white trembling hand in his old wrinkled one, he led her up on the platform by his side.

"Must tell Cherokees you want their help," Uncle Ned said softly.

Mandie looked at him and smiled. She could do that.

"My people," she began in a weak, shaky voice. "Please help me find my dear friend, Joe Woodard. The same terrible people who have been tearing down the walls of your hospital have taken my friend." Her voice grew stronger as she continued. "We must find Joe first, and then catch the crooks. We must put a stop to their destructive work and get the hospital built before someone really needs it. Will you help me, please?"

She paused, and Uncle Ned translated her speech into Cherokee. Instantly, the Indians stood and applauded wildly, stomping their feet and chanting.

Tears glistened in Mandie's eyes as she smiled and motioned for them to sit down.

"Thank you, my people, thank you!" she cried. "I know some of y'all know Dr. Woodard, Joe's father, but I want him to come up here and let everyone meet him. Dr. Woodard?"

While Uncle Ned translated, Mandie motioned for Dr. Woodard to join her. Dr. Woodard looked startled, but after an awkward silence, he got to his feet and walked rapidly to the platform.

"I know a white man is not supposed to speak at a council meeting, but Dr. Woodard is no ordinary white man," Mandie began again, pausing after every few words for Uncle Ned to translate. "First of all, he's Joe's father and he is the best friend the Cherokees ever had. Without his doctoring, many Cherokees would have died. And he will be in charge of the hospital when it is finished. Now, here he is," she said.

When Uncle Ned finished translating, the crowd again stood, this time to welcome the doctor. Then they sat back down.

Beads of sweat formed on Dr. Woodard's brow as he stepped forward nervously. "Thank you, my dear friends," he said loudly. Uncle Ned translated again. "I know you will do everything possible to find my son, Joe. I have faith in you. And when the person or persons responsible for destroying the hospital walls is caught, I hope you mete out a stiff punishment. Thank you."

As the crowd again clapped, and stomped, and beat on the boards of the benches, Mandie turned to Uncle Ned. "May we sit down now?" she asked.

"Go, sit, Papoose. Doctor, sit," he said, smiling.

When Mandie and Dr. Woodard had returned to their seats, Uncle Ned quieted the crowd. "Now we vote to find Joe," he said in both Cherokee and English, obviously wanting everyone present to know what was happening. "Everyone who say yes raise hand."

It looked as though all the Cherokees in the audience raised their hands except Tsa'ni and the boys with him.

"Now everyone who say no raise hand," the old man said.

There was complete silence. Mandie turned slightly and gasped as Tsa'ni and the two boys raised their hands.

Uncle Ned looked directly at the boys in disgust. "Why you raise hand no?" he asked.

The three stood up.

Tsa'ni spoke in English. "We think the Cherokee gods are tearing down the hospital and would not like our interference."

Everyone stared at him in silence.

"No Cherokee gods," Uncle Ned said angrily. "Only one God, Big God. You know that."

"That is what the white man wants you to believe," Tsa'ni replied. "Do not forget the Big God is the white man's God."

Mandie jumped up. "That is not so, Tsa'ni, and you know it!" she yelled. "There is only one God. You are just trying to confuse things. I think you are the one who is tearing down the walls. And I believe you also know what happened to Joe."

"I am not tearing down walls," Tsa'ni argued. "But if I knew who it was, I would help them destroy the white man's building. And Joe got lost somewhere because he is not man enough to take care of himself," the Indian boy scoffed.

Trembling with anger, Uncle Ned yelled at Tsa'ni in Cherokee. Mandie couldn't understand but Tsa'ni did. He plopped down on the bench and said no more.

Mandie sat down and looked at Sallie. "What did Uncle Ned say to him?" she asked.

"He said unless Tsa'ni repents and believes in the Big God, his soul will burn in hell forever," Sallie explained. "And if he is involved in this crime in any way, he will be severely punished."

As Uncle Ned continued to speak in Cherokee, Dimar told her that Uncle Ned was explaining how to go about the search.

Finally Uncle Ned stepped to the edge of the platform and raised his hand. He said something softly in Cherokee, and the crowd stood. Looking toward Mandie and then the sky, he said loudly in English, "Big God, we ask help to find doctor boy and to stop crook." Then he began praying in Cherokee so the people could understand him.

They all raised their faces upward.

Mandie squeezed Sallie's hand on one side and Dimar's on the other as she prayed silently, *Dear God, please help us find Joe. Guide our footsteps in the right direction, and help us stop the crooks from tearing down the hospital. I know you will help us. You always do. I love you, dear God. Amen.*

As the meeting broke up, Mandie felt a heavy burden lift from her heart. She knew God would answer her prayers. She didn't know how but she knew she could depend on Him.

Chapter 8 / Trouble for Mandie and Sallie

Just as Mandie came out of the council house, Uncle Wirt grabbed Tsa'ni by the shoulders and shook him so hard his head wobbled. The whole time he was screaming at his grandson in Cherokee.

Everyone stood back watching. No one spoke.

Uncle Ned stepped forward and laid a hand on Uncle Wirt's arm. "Must go now," Uncle Ned told him. "Go search."

Uncle Wirt dropped his hands and nodded in assent. Tsa'ni quickly turned to leave.

"Tsa'ni," Mandie called to him. "I still believe you know where Joe is, and if you don't tell us, you're going to be awfully sorry."

"Ask your Big God where he is. You say He knows everything," Tsa'ni called back, disappearing into the crowd.

"He is a bad Cherokee," Sallie repeated.

"He does not like white people," Dimar said. "He is afraid they will change the way of life for the Cherokees. He does not realize the Cherokees must learn better ways of living."

"I think the hospital will be the best thing that ever happened to the Cherokees," Sallie said.

"We'll get it built in spite of all this trouble," Mandie assured them. "God will help us."

Elizabeth caught up with Mandie as the young people walked toward Uncle Ned's wagon. "I am proud of you, Amanda," Elizabeth told her daughter. "That was an impressive speech you made. I know the Cherokees will find Joe, wherever he is."

"Thank you, Mother," Mandie said, smiling up at her. "May I go with the Cherokees on their search?"

"I don't think they will want you to, Amanda. Your Uncle John says that the men will begin first, and if necessary the women will join in later, and then maybe the children," her mother said.

"But, Mother, when the women join in, I should also help," Mandie argued.

"We'll talk about it later, dear," said Elizabeth, starting toward Uncle Wirt's wagon.

Mandie followed her mother and climbed into Uncle Ned's wagon with Sallie and Dimar. As she sat down, Mandie let out a big sigh.

Sallie patted Mandie's hand. "I know you are disappointed, Mandie, but it is better this way," Sallie tried to comfort her friend.

"The men can move faster without the women," Dimar added. "And I promise to let you know the minute we find Joe."

"You're going with Uncle Ned and the men?" Mandie asked.

"Yes. As soon as we take y'all home, we will meet the other men at the hospital and start searching from there," the Indian boy explained.

"But you aren't really a full-grown man, Dimar," Mandie teased.

"The Cherokees consider me a man. I am now thirteen years old," Dimar said solemnly.

Just then Uncle Ned came and helped Morning Star onto the seat of the wagon. Then he harnessed his horses.

Climbing into the wagon, he looked at the young people. "We hurry now. We go home," he said. Picking up the reins, he turned the wagon onto the road.

Mandie was sitting in the wagon bed behind Uncle Ned. "Thank you, Uncle Ned," she called to him. "Thank you for asking all the Cherokees to join in the search for Joe."

"Doctor boy friend of Papoose. I promise Jim Shaw I watch over Papoose when he go to happy hunting ground," the old man explained. "We find doctor boy for sad Papoose."

Mandie smiled. "Thank you, Uncle Ned. I love every one of those Cherokee people. After all, they are my people, too."

Sallie gave Mandie a hug. "We all love you, too, Mandie."

Dimar smiled at her. "Yes, we do."

Mandie blushed. Dimar was good-looking and awfully nice. She looked down.

Dimar sensed her discomfort. "We will find Joe for you," he promised. "And the crooks, too."

"Thank you, Dimar. You are truly a friend," Mandie said.

"If I am in the group that finds Joe, I will let you know myself, I promise," he said.

Uncle Ned looked back at Mandie. "If I find doctor boy I bring him to Papoose," he called to her over the rattle of the wagon. "We hurry fast." He whipped the reins, and the horses sped off down the road.

When they reached Uncle Ned's house, Morning Star ran into the cabin and quickly began packing food for the men.

Uncle Ned was already unharnessing the horses by the time Uncle Wirt and his wagonload had arrived. Elizabeth went inside to help Morning Star, and the girls stood around in the way, not knowing what to do.

Dimar brought fresh horses from the pasture for the three men and himself and tethered them at the door. The girls went outside to wait with him until the men came outside and prepared to leave.

"Please be careful," Mandie called to them as they mounted their horses.

"We will," Uncle John promised.

Elizabeth stood with Morning Star in the doorway. "I wish you all Godspeed," she said, waving to them.

"Dr. Woodard," Mandie called, "I'll be praying that you find Joe soon and that he is all right."

"Bless you, Amanda," the doctor answered.

Uncle Ned took command. "We go now. We find Joe. "Find crooks," he said. And with that, the four were off, riding quickly down the dirt road.

The women and girls watched until the men were out of sight and all they could see was a cloud of dust. Then they went back into the cabin to wait.

The day dragged by for the girls. They ate the noon meal. They helped with the chores. They wandered listlessly around the yard until late afternoon. Then they sat on a fallen log under the big chestnut tree.

"I wish they would hurry back so we'd know something," Mandie said.

"You know they will return just as soon as they find Joe," Sallie replied.

Mandie sighed. "I know, but I wish I could do something."

"Would you like to pick some wild flowers?" Sallie asked.

"Sure." Mandie stood. "But I'll have to ask Mother first."

They ran for the cabin and found Elizabeth peeling potatoes. Morning Star was stirring several pots over the fire in the fireplace.

"Mother, why are you cooking so much food?" Mandie asked.

"We don't know when the men will return, Amanda," Elizabeth replied, "or how many there will be, so we have to cook a lot of food and have it ready for them."

"You don't need us, do you?" Mandie asked.

"No, dear. Morning Star and I have everything under control," her mother said.

"Then could Sallie and I go out and pick some wild flowers?" Mandie asked.

"If you promise not to be gone too long," Elizabeth consented. "It's not long till suppertime."

"We won't," Mandie promised.

"Come on, Mandie," Sallie said after talking to Morning Star. "I have permission to go."

As the girls hurried outdoors and started down the road, Snowball followed.

"We can go to the woods," Sallie suggested. "It is not very far."

"Are there a lot of flowers there?" Mandie asked.

"Yes, everywhere. All kinds," Sallie told her.

At the bend in the road, the girls walked off into the

woods. Sallie was right. As they went along, they found more and more flowers. Pulling their aprons up to hold the flowers, they kept going, not realizing how late it was getting.

Then Sallie stopped suddenly and looked around. "Mandie, we are a long way into the woods. We are almost to the hospital," Sallie said.

"We are?" said Mandie. "But it took a long time to get there on the road."

"It is much shorter through the woods," Sallie said. "But since we—" she paused, listening. "Mandie, do you hear something?"

Mandie held her breath to listen for a moment. "I hear pounding," she said.

"Yes, it sounds like someone chopping wood," Sallie added.

"Chopping wood? And we are near the hospital? Could it be the workmen who are building the hospital?" Mandie asked.

"We will go find out," Sallie replied.

The two girls hurried on through the woods, still holding their flowers in their aprons. The noise grew louder, and then it suddenly ceased. The girls stopped and looked at each other. The sound of footsteps came toward them through the brush.

"Quick! Behind those big trees!" said Sallie, running for cover.

Mandie followed. Together they stood there, holding their breath, waiting to see who came along. Mandie's heart beat wildly. The footsteps grew louder. Three men carrying axes passed in front of them, then walked on out of sight.

The girls, shaking with fright, came out from behind the trees.

"Who was that?" Mandie asked.

"That was the Catawba man, Running Fire, and his sons. He is the husband of Moongo, the old Cherokee woman who came back not long ago. She had been gone many, many years, but they now live in an old barn near here," Sallie explained.

"Oh, yes," Mandie replied. "Uncle Ned told us about them. But they were all three carrying axes, and the chopping noise stopped just before they came by here," Mandie observed. "Come on! Hurry! Let's check the hospital."

"This way," Sallie told her, quickly running ahead.

When they came to the hospital clearing, they were panting for breath. They stared at the hospital, then at each other. The workmen were gone, and the walls had all been chopped down.

"Sallie, let's follow them!" Mandie urged her friend. Turning back the way they had come, Mandie held Snowball tightly as they ran. Since the men weren't walking very fast, the girls quickly caught up with them.

Angrily Mandie ran up to Running Fire and stood in front of him, blocking his path.

"You tore down the walls to the hospital, didn't you?" she cried. "Why did you do that? Why?" she demanded, tears choking her voice.

"Move!" Running Fire demanded.

Mandie stepped closer. "You also kidnapped Joe, didn't you? Where is he? Where is he?" Mandie screamed, dropping her apron and spilling the flowers to the ground.

Sallie also dropped her flowers and grabbed Mandie's arm. "Come, Mandie," she said.

Mandie ignored her friend.

"Well, you won't get away with it!" she shouted. "We have the whole Cherokee nation out looking for you."

The Catawba man reached out and grabbed her long blonde braid. "We take you, too," he said. Then pointing to Sallie, he told his sons, "Get her!"

The two younger men snatched Sallie and held her tight.

"Go," ordered Running Fire, pushing Mandie ahead of him. "We take you where white boy is."

The other two men pushed Sallie along with them.

Mandie held Snowball tightly. "You don't have to shove. We'll go," said Mandie. "If you're taking us to Joe, we'll go."

"Shut up!" snapped Running Fire.

Without another word, the girls went along with the three men to the old barn where the Catawba man lived.

"Stop here!" Running Fire ordered. Then turning to one of his sons, he said, "Open."

The younger man, after waiting to be sure his brother had a secure hold on Sallie, walked to a mound of straw and kicked it aside. Beneath the straw was a wooden door made flat into the ground. He removed a large boulder sitting on the door, then pulled the door open.

The girls watched in amazement. No wonder no one had been able to find Joe if he was in there.

Running Fire motioned to the girls. "Get in!" he ordered, shoving Mandie toward the opening in the ground.

The son pushed Sallie forward.

Mandie looked down into the dark hole and saw an old ladder hanging down inside.

"Get in!" Running Fire shouted again, giving Mandie a sharp push.

Trembling with fear and anger, Mandie stooped down, put Snowball on her shoulder, and then carefully made her way down the ladder into the storm cellar. Sallie was forced to follow.

At the bottom, when Mandie's feet touched ground, she peered around the semidarkness. Someone groaned. Over in the corner Joe lay on the ground, gagged and tied up. Mandie ran to him, and Sallie quickly joined her.

"Joe!" Mandie cried, fumbling to untie him. "Joe! It's me, Mandie!"

The boy only groaned.

The girls looked him over. He was bruised, and beaten, and evidently very ill, almost unconscious.

Overhead, Running Fire closed the wooden door, and the girls heard the stone being pushed back over it.

Mandie bent over Joe compassionately. "Sallie, what are we going to do?" she cried. "Joe is sick."

"He is cold, too," Sallie said. "It is cold in here."

Mandie stood up. "Let's use our aprons to cover him up a little," she told Sallie.

The two girls quickly removed their big, full aprons and carefully covered the boy as well as they could.

With the door closed, it was almost completely dark in the storm cellar.

Mandie shivered. "Sallie, we must pray. Joe is sick, and if he doesn't get help soon, he may die," she said with tears in her eyes. "He's been gone since night before last."

The two girls quietly knelt beside Joe and looked upward.

"Dear God, please, please get us out of here," Mandie prayed aloud. "Let somebody find us before it's too late for Joe. Please don't let him die, dear God, please." Mandie's voice broke. She took a deep breath and repeated her favorite prayer from the Bible. "What time I am afraid,

I will trust in Thee." She began to sob.

"Yes, dear God, please do not wait too long," Sallie begged.

Sallie put her arm around her friend. "Mandie, remember what Dr. Woodard said. We must not give up. We must not!" the Indian girl told her.

Mandie rubbed her sleeve across her wet eyes and straightened up. "We won't give up. Never!" Mandie determined. "Someone will find us. I know they will."

"Yes, someone will find us," Sallie agreed.

Mandie sat quietly for a moment, thinking. "Sallie, I've just realized something awful," she said.

"What?"

"I'm afraid I have wrongly accused Tsa'ni," Mandie cried. "He was not the one who was tearing down the walls."

"You can straighten things out with Tsa'ni later," the Indian girl replied.

"But I accused him in the council house in front of all our people," Mandie reminded her. "He'll never forgive me. I just hope God will."

"If you ask God to forgive you, I think Tsa'ni will, too," Sallie comforted her. "But we must get out of this place first."

"I hope it is soon," Mandie replied.

Chapter 9 / Tsa'ni Tells a Lie

The day was beginning to fade away. Elizabeth and Morning Star sat near the open doorway where they could watch for the others to return.

Elizabeth fidgeted nervously. "Morning Star, I know you can't understand much of what I say, but I have to talk to someone," she said. "I am worried. Amanda and Sallie should have been back long ago. They only went to pick flowers. And someone in the search party should have let us know something by now. Do you understand what I am saying, Morning Star?"

Morning Star grunted and nodded her head. "Late," she said, frowning.

"That's right. You do understand some things," said Elizabeth, a little relieved. "I don't know which way they went, but even if I went to look for them they might come back a different way." She pulled out a handkerchief and dabbed at her eyes. "Oh, why did I give Amanda permission to pick flowers? There is so much danger around with Joe missing and the hospital vandalism."

Morning Star listened intently. To Elizabeth's surprise, the old Indian squaw stood up and said, "We find. We go."

"No, Morning Star," Elizabeth objected. "We don't know which way they went."

"Flowers, woods," Morning Star tried to explain.

"You mean they went into the woods to pick flowers? Is that where they went?"

The old woman nodded.

"But the woods are—"

"We go," Morning Star repeated.

"Wait," Elizabeth said. "I must leave a note in case someone comes before we get back."

She walked across the room and rummaged in her travel bag for a piece of paper and a pencil. Morning Star watched her in puzzlement.

As Elizabeth sat down at the table to write the note, a shadow blocked the light from the doorway. Elizabeth looked up to see Tsa'ni standing there.

Tsa'ni stared at her without speaking.

When Morning Star saw him, she began talking rapidly to him in Cherokee. Tsa'ni listened in surprise as Elizabeth sat and watched. Evidently the old woman was telling him about the girls.

Tsa'ni looked at Elizabeth. "Mrs. Shaw, Morning Star says Mandie and Sallie went out to pick flowers and have not come back."

Elizabeth got up and walked toward the boy. "Yes, Tsa'ni, that is true. We are worried sick. Something must have happened to them," Elizabeth said.

Impatiently, Morning Star rushed over to the boy and shook him, obviously scolding him harshly in Cherokee.

Elizabeth waited to see what the vile-tempered boy would do.

Tsa'ni said something to the old squaw then turned

back to Elizabeth. "She wants me to go hunt them," he said belligerently.

"Oh, Tsa'ni, would you?" Elizabeth pleaded. "Morning Star and I were about to go and look for them when you came in, but we don't know where to look. Morning Star said they went into the woods. You probably know this area better than she does, and I know nothing at all about it. Will you go?" she repeated.

Tsa'ni scuffed the toe of his mocassin on the rough floor and lowered his eyes. Elizabeth Shaw had always been kind to him, even when all the others were not. He could promise to look for them, but it didn't matter to him whether he found them or not. If he found the girls he would tell them to go home. If he didn't find them, he would just keep on going. He had only come by Uncle Ned's house to see if his grandfather had returned.

"I will look for them," he told Elizabeth. Turning to Morning Star, he spoke rapidly in Cherokee.

The old woman smiled.

"Tsa'ni, thank you. I appreciate it," Elizabeth said sincerely. "I certainly hope you find them. And, please, don't you get lost, too."

"I have never been lost. I know every tree in the woods," the boy bragged. "I will go now."

He hurried out into the yard and started down the road. The women watched him until he was out of sight.

Tsa'ni took his time tramping through the woods. He headed straight for the hospital building, looked around there, and then circled out away from it. Enlarging the circle as he walked, he came nearer and nearer the Catawba man's house.

Then noticing something white through the bushes, he made his way through the brush and found the two piles of flowers the girls had dropped. He bent down, examining the flowers and the tracks around them. Evidently there had been three men here besides the girls. His heartbeat quickened. Three men were more than he wanted to take on. He stood up, looked around, and continued on through the woods. He would just go on home. It was getting late.

As Tsa'ni walked quickly through the deepest part of the woods, he suddenly spotted his grandfather's search party through the trees. Tsa'ni tried to escape notice, but the old Indian saw him.

"Come!" Uncle Wirt called to him.

Knowing he had to obey, Tsa'ni slowly walked over to his grandfather. The others in the party heard Uncle Wirt's shout and came to join him.

"Where you go?" his grandfather demanded.

"Home," Tsa'ni replied.

"Where been?" the old Indian persisted.

Tsa'ni hesitated.

Uncle Ned stepped forward. "To my house?" he asked.

"Yes," the boy answered.

"Why?" Uncle Wirt asked.

"To see if you had come back," Tsa'ni replied. "For what other reason would I go there?"

John Shaw looked concerned. "Was everyone there all right?" he asked.

"Yes," the boy said sharply.

Dimar looked at Tsa'ni with suspicion. He didn't appear to believe anything Tsa'ni said.

"Did you see anyone else in the woods?" Dr. Woodard asked.

Tsa'ni looked at the doctor coldly and then answered, "Of course not."

"We go back," Uncle Ned told them. "Crooks not this way. Crooks that way." He pointed toward the trail to the hospital.

"You're right, Uncle Ned," John agreed. "If they had come this way we would have seen them."

Dimar looked over at Dr. Woodard. The old man was tired and worried about his son. "Dr. Woodard, when we find the crooks, I am sure we will find Joe," he said. "I think the crooks hid Joe somewhere."

"Yes, Dimar, that's what I've been thinking, too," the doctor answered.

As Uncle Ned led the way back to the hospital site, the other men followed. Tsa'ni stood there watching them for a minute, then continued on his way home.

When the sky became dark and Tsa'ni didn't return to Uncle Ned's cabin, Elizabeth and Morning Star paced the floor frantically. Evidently the girls had not been found.

Chapter 10 / Snowball Helps

Mandie and Sallie huddled together in the storm cellar, trying to comfort one another while they watched over Joe. How they wished someone would come and rescue them!

Suddenly there was a noise overhead. The girls quickly jumped up, and Snowball slid off Mandie's lap.

"I heard something," Mandie whispered.

"Someone is at the door overhead," Sallie replied.

"I'm going to climb the ladder and surprise them when they open the door," Mandie said softly.

"Please be careful," Sallie pleaded. "We do not know if it is the crooks or our people."

Mandie climbed the ladder and stopped near the door above. Slowly the door was opened a crack, and Running Fire's face appeared in the opening. His beady eyes looked at her, then glanced down at Sallie and Joe.

"Mister, please let us out of here," Mandie begged. "My friend Joe is sick. He needs a doctor bad."

"No," the Catawba man snapped. "We wait. We catch white men."

"Please don't harm anyone else," Mandie said. "We

don't even know why you hate us so."

"White man must go home. Leave us alone," said Running Fire. "Hospital not good for Indian."

"But the Cherokees all want the hospital to be built," Mandie argued, hanging on to the ladder. "They want to be able to take their sick there."

"No!" Running Fire stormed. "No! Hospital not be built! Not need white man's doctor. I am medicine man. I heal sick Indians. Not need white man. No, no, no!"

Sallie called to him from below. "You are a medicine man for the Catawbas. Cherokees do not want a Catawba medicine man. We want a white doctor who knows how to heal."

"No, no, no!" Running Fire shook with anger as he perched over the doorway. "Medicine man doctor all Indians."

"So you are a medicine man. Now I understand what's been going on," Mandie said. "You are angry because the Cherokees do not believe in medicine men anymore. They have seen white doctors heal their sick. They do not need you."

"Hush up!" the Catawba man cried. "I come down and hush you up."

As he fumbled trying to close the door, Mandie spied a good-sized rock lying near the top of the ladder. Grabbing the rock quickly, she stuck it under the door just as Running Fire shut it. The rock let a crack of dim light into the dark cellar. Mandie listened. Running Fire rolled the boulder on top of the cellar entrance again, but the rock held the door open a crack.

Mandie slid down the ladder. "Look, Sallie!" she whispered. "I put a rock under the door so it wouldn't shut tight."

Sallie glanced upward. "That was fast thinking. Now we have a little light and air in here. But it will soon be dark outside and then it will be pitch black in here again," she said.

Mandie bent over Joe in the faint light from above. His face was all bloody and bruised. Their aprons still covered his motionless body.

"Joe has not moved an inch," Mandie said.

"He is still breathing though," Sallie replied.

Mandie picked up his limp, cold hand and rubbed it with hers. "Sallie, we've got to get him out of here before it's too late," she cried.

"I wish I could think of a way," Sallie replied.

Snowball rubbed around Mandie's legs and meowed loudly. Evidently he was hungry.

Picking him up, Mandie rubbed his soft white fur and put his cold nose against her cheek. "Snowball, I'm sorry you're hungry. Come to think of it, I am, too," she told the kitten.

"So am I," Sallie said. "My grandmother and your mother must have supper ready by now. I know they are worried about us."

"I imagine Mother is walking the floor," Mandie told her friend.

"My grandmother is probably out looking for us," Sallie said.

Mandie thought for a moment. "You're right. Mother and Morning Star are both out looking for us, I'm sure," Mandie said. "Oh, will my mother be angry with me!"

"I think they will be too glad to see us to be angry with us," Sallie told her.

"I hope you're right," Mandie replied. "I'm going up the ladder again to see if I can see anything through that crack," Mandie said, putting Snowball on her shoulder.

Climbing the rungs of the ladder, Mandie got as close to the crack as she could and tried to see outside. But the crack was at an angle, so she couldn't see much.

Snowball jumped onto the ledge under the door and began scratching at the dirt around the crack.

Mandie reached for him. "Snowball, come back here," she scolded.

Snowball only scratched harder, kicking dust in Mandie's eyes.

That gave Mandie an idea. "Sallie," she called to her friend. "If we could scratch enough dirt away, we could poke Snowball through the hole. Then maybe he would go home."

Sallie stood up. "That is a good idea. Is the ladder strong enough to hold both of us?"

"I think so," Mandie said. "It didn't shake when I came up. Here, I'll move over to one side."

As Mandie moved over, Sallie carefully climbed the ladder. It did not even sway.

Arriving at the top, Sallie looked at the crack where Snowball was still scratching. "Yes, I think we can make the hole larger so Snowball can get through," she agreed. "But there is nothing to dig with."

Pushing the kitten aside on the ledge, Mandie and Sallie went to work on the dirt with their bare hands. They broke their fingernails and scratched their hands, but they kept digging. The hole slowly grew a little larger. The girls stopped and listened now and then to be sure no one was around to hear them.

"Whew!" Mandie sighed. "My fingers are bleeding."

Sallie looked at her own hands. "Mine, too," she said.

"But now the hole is almost large enough for Snowball to go through."

Leaning back, Mandie looked at the hole and then at Snowball. "Come here, Snowball," she called, reaching out to him. She held him up next to the hole and looked at Sallie. "It's large enough."

"Are you sure? Do not force him through. It might hurt him," Sallie cautioned.

Mandie looked again. "Maybe just a little bit more."

The girls dug more dirt out until the hole finally looked large enough.

"Now!" Mandie declared.

"Yes," Sallie agreed.

Mandie picked up Snowball and started to push him through the hole. Then she stopped suddenly. "I have an idea," she cried. "Let's tie our hair ribbons around Snowball. Then whoever finds him might figure out that we are not able to come home."

"That is a good idea," Sallie said, quickly pulling the red ribbon from her long, straight black hair.

Mandie untied the blue ribbon from her blonde braid and started to tie it around Snowball's neck.

Sallie stopped her. "No, no," she said. "He might get caught on something and the ribbon would choke him. Tie it around his belly."

"Will it stay?"

"If you tie it like this it will," Sallie said, showing Mandie how to crisscross it behind Snowball's front legs.

"Perfect," said Mandie, tying her ribbon as Sallie had shown her.

Snowball thought it was a game. Meowing, he rolled over on his back, trying to reach the ribbons with his claws.

"No, silly cat," Mandie scolded him. "Don't pull it off. You've got to be our messenger to get us out of here."

She picked him up and tried to push him through the hole. Snowball didn't like that at all, and Sallie had to help. Then when he got outside, he tried to come back in. Mandie quickly stuffed a rock in the hole to make it too small for him to get through. But Snowball didn't leave. He just sat outside and meowed loudly.

"Goodness!" Mandie exclaimed. "He'll alarm the whole neighborhood. Those crooks will hear him and come to see what's going on."

"Maybe we could get him back inside," Sallie suggested.

"Let's try," Mandie agreed.

Removing the rock, they tried to coax the kitten inside. But he only sniffed at their hands and meowed louder.

"Well, I guess we'll just have to wait and see who hears him," Mandie said, disappointed.

"Yes, that is all we can do," Sallie agreed. "I am going back down. I want to sit for a while.

"I'll stay up here and listen," Mandie told her friend.

While Sallie kept watch over Joe, Mandie listened at the cellar door. Someone was sure to come soon. Snowball wouldn't quit meowing.

Chapter 11 / Rescue

Tsa'ni was almost home when he decided to go back.
If he circled far enough out, he could bypass his grand-
father's search party and get back to Uncle Ned's cabin.
He might as well tell the women he didn't find the girls.
He wouldn't mention that he had met the search party.

As Tsa'ni tried to sneak past the Catawba man's house,
he suddenly heard Snowball crying. Silently he moved
closer to see the kitten. There was Snowball, sitting by
the barn, decorated with ribbons, howling for no apparent
reason. Tsa'ni decided that the cat must have gotten lost.

When Snowball saw Tsa'ni approaching, he hunched
up, ruffled his fur, and hissed at the boy.

Tsa'ni quickly jumped back. He had never touched
that cat before, and he didn't intend to now.

As Tsa'ni turned and quietly continued on his way,
Mandie stood at the top of the cellar ladder, holding her
breath.

"Sallie, there was someone outside just now," she
whispered. "Snowball stopped his meowing and began
hissing at somebody. It must have been somebody he
didn't like."

"Yes, I heard," Sallie called softly from below. "But whoever it was must have left. Snowball is meowing again."

As Tsa'ni headed for Uncle Ned's cabin, he began making up the tale he would tell the women.

Elizabeth and Morning Star saw him approaching and stood in the doorway to wait.

"I saw no one in the woods," he told them as he entered the cabin. "No one at all." He repeated it in Cherokee to Morning Star.

"Oh dear!" Elizabeth exclaimed.

Morning Star began screaming at the boy in Cherokee, but Tsa'ni just stood there with a sly grin on his face.

Elizabeth watched, trying to understand. "What did Morning Star say?" she asked as the squaw stomped over to the table and began wrapping up some food.

"She told me I should have found them. She said that I am no good, so she is going to find them," Tsa'ni told Elizabeth.

Elizabeth walked over to Morning Star, watching her put some food into a basket.

"I am going with you," Elizabeth announced. "Tsa'ni, will you go with us?"

Tsa'ni hesitated. "Yes," he said. "I will go with you. I will get the lantern and the matches. It will be dark soon."

"I need to get a coat," said Elizabeth. "Tsa'ni, will you please tell Morning Star to get a coat or something warm. It will be cold before long. And tell her that you and I are going with her."

Tsa'ni walked over to Morning Star and spoke quickly in Cherokee. Morning Star replied but kept wrapping food to fill the basket. Then she reached for a jar, filled it with water, and set it up straight in the basket so it wouldn't spill.

Tsa'ni took a lantern from the nail where it hung by the door and put some matches in his pocket.

Elizabeth finished the note she had started writing earlier, and placed it in the middle of the long table. The three left the cabin and walked down the road toward the woods.

Silently, Elizabeth again prayed that the girls were safe and asked God's help in finding them.

Morning Star, sensing that Elizabeth was praying, raised her eyes toward the sky and said her prayer in Cherokee.

In the meantime, Uncle Ned had led the search party back into the woods. Although it was getting dark, they didn't light their lanterns for fear the crooks would see the light. They all walked quietly. Only occasionally was there a sound of a twig breaking under someone's foot.

Uncle Ned stopped for a moment, pointing ahead to the left. "Near Catawba man's house," he muttered softly.

"Let's see if anyone is home," John suggested.

"Yes, but quiet," Uncle Ned reminded them, stealthily leading the group forward.

The old barn came into view when they reached the clearing. The men slowly slipped around the makeshift house and peered through the open window.

"No one is home," Dr. Woodard whispered.

"I go inside," said Uncle Wirt.

"I suppose we should search every conceivable place," John agreed. "They could have hidden Joe anywhere."

Uncle Wirt quietly opened the sagging door and slipped inside. The others watched through the window as the old man searched the room inside. He looked under everything and behind everything. There wasn't much furniture in the old one-room barn.

"We go around," Uncle Ned said, waving his arms to indicate searching the surrounding area.

As the men fanned out in various directions, Uncle Ned headed straight toward the storm cellar. The old Indian heard a noise and stopped to listen. He walked a little farther. It sounded like someone crying. Uncle Ned hurried forward and found Snowball sitting there, meowing.

He looked around quickly, then stooped and picked up the white kitten. Snowball immediately hushed and started purring. Uncle Ned examined the ribbons tied around the kitten.

"Snowball, where Papoose? What you do in woods?" the old man talked to the kitten, smoothing its white fur.

Although there wasn't much light and the Catawbas had camouflaged the storm cellar door, Uncle Ned's sharp eyes noticed the small hole in the ground. He stooped to look closer.

Hovering over the hole, he once again talked to the kitten. "Snowball, hole there," he said, setting the kitten down. He kicked at the mound of straw and found the wooden door to the storm cellar.

Mandie's heart beat wildly. "Someone is outside, Sallie," she whispered.

Sallie quickly climbed up the ladder and stood beside her friend.

Uncle Ned stooped to move the boulder on top of the door. "Move, Snowball," he said, giving the boulder a push.

Instantly Mandie and Sallie recognized the voice.

"Uncle Ned!" Mandie cried.

"Grandfather!" called Sallie.

Uncle Ned realized who was inside. "Papooses, what

you do in there?" he shouted.

Standing up, he signalled the other men with a shrill bird whistle, then struggled to pull the cellar door open.

Uncle John, Dr. Woodard, Uncle Wirt, and Dimar came running at his call.

"Papooses in there," Uncle Ned told them.

"Papooses? Amanda and Sallie?" Uncle John asked.

When the door finally came open, the girls were clinging to the top of the ladder. Everyone started talking at once.

Mandie grabbed the doctor's sleeve. "Dr. Woodard, Joe is down there. He's sick—bad," she said as she and Sallie climbed out.

Dimar quickly jumped into the cellar, and Dr. Woodard made his way down the ladder.

"Joe, at last," Uncle John said with relief. He called down to Dr. Woodard. "Need me to help, or would I be in the way?"

"We will manage," Dr. Woodard called back.

In a few minutes Dimar appeared on the ladder with Joe's limp body slung over his shoulder. Dr. Woodard came right behind him, carrying the girls' aprons. Reaching the top, they laid Joe on the ground, and again covered him with the aprons.

"Go get blanket," Uncle Ned directed Dimar, pointing back toward Running Fire's house.

Dimar hurried off, and Uncle Wirt followed in case he had any trouble.

As Dr. Woodard examined his unconscious son, Mandie and Sallie explained how they got there.

Mandie clung to Uncle John, while Sallie hugged her grandfather.

"The Catawba man, Running Fire, is the one who has

been tearing down the hospital," Mandie told them. "He's a medicine man."

"That explains a lot of things," said Dr. Woodard.

Mandie knelt beside Joe, watching the doctor work. "Will he be all right, Dr. Woodard?" she asked, trembling. In the dim light, she could again see the dried blood and bruises on Joe's ashen face.

A tired, worried frown creased the doctor's forehead. "We'll see," he said. "We must get him in a warm bed at once."

Dimar and Uncle Wirt returned with two heavy blankets.

"We make bed," Uncle Ned told them. Laying one blanket on the ground, he waited for Dr. Woodard to move Joe onto it. Uncle Ned covered Joe with the other blanket, then motioned to Uncle Wirt, Uncle John and Dimar to help him pick up the corners to form a hammock-like bed for carrying Joe.

Dr. Woodard protested being left out of the operation. "I could carry one corner," he said.

"No, it's better you stay right alongside him," Uncle John replied as the party started off through the woods, carrying the sick boy to Uncle Ned's house.

Chapter 12 / Captured!

Tsa'ni carried the lantern as he led Morning Star and Elizabeth to the hospital site. They met no one and heard nothing. Now and then they stopped to call the girls' names, but received no answer.

Elizabeth was becoming frantic. She wished she knew how to contact John to get his help.

While Tsa'ni and the women were searching the woods, the men arrived at Uncle Ned's house with Joe. When they entered the cabin, they looked around but found no one home.

"Where is Elizabeth? And Morning Star?" Uncle John said. "Elizabeth! Elizabeth!" he called up the ladder to the attic room. No answer. "Now don't tell me they've disappeared, too," he said.

Mandie quickly climbed the ladder, looked around, and came back down. Then she saw the note on the table. She ran to pick it up. "Uncle John, they've gone to look for Sallie and me," she said, handing him the note.

"Of all things," said Uncle John, reading the note. "We can't seem to get all of us together. It's dark out there now. There's no telling where they are."

Uncle Ned helped Dr. Woodard put Joe in one of the beds near the fireplace, then stirred up the fire. "Morning Star know woods. Not get lost," he said.

"But it's getting late, Uncle Ned. We'd better go find them," Uncle John said.

"Yes, we find," Uncle Wirt spoke up.

"I will go, too," Dimar volunteered.

"Amanda, you and Sallie be sure you stay right here with Dr. Woodard," said Uncle John. "Don't set foot out of this house for any reason at all. Do you hear me?"

"Yes, sir, I understand," Mandie replied meekly. "I'm sorry we caused so much trouble. We won't ever go looking for flowers again."

"I am sorry, too," Sallie added.

"Dr. Woodard may need your help with Joe anyway," said Uncle John. "We'll be back as soon as we find your mother and Morning Star."

Uncle Wirt gave Dr. Woodard a rifle. "Catawba man come, you shoot," he said.

"Well, I'll sure slow him up with this if he comes messing around here," Dr. Woodard replied. He stood the rifle by the bed and turned back to Joe. "Girls, will you get me a pan of hot water?"

"Sure, Dr. Woodard," Mandie answered, quickly obeying.

As Uncle John and the others left, Sallie closed the door behind them and put the crossbar in place.

When Mandie returned with the hot water, Dr. Woodard bathed his son's wounds and applied some medicine. Then he placed a hot brick at the bottom of Joe's bed to keep his feet warm.

Joe remained unconscious, and Dr. Woodard stayed right by the bed.

The men hadn't been gone long when they spotted a lighted lantern ahead.

"That must be them," said Uncle John. "No one else would be going around with a lighted lantern when we've all been trying to catch up with those crooks."

As the men moved closer, they saw the two women and Tsa'ni searching the bushes.

"Tsa'ni told us he was going home when we saw him," Uncle John said, confused.

"Tsa'ni!" Uncle Wirt called.

Tsa'ni and the women stopped and looked around. The men quickly came within the light of the lantern.

Elizabeth ran to John, and he eagerly wrapped his arms around her.

"Oh, John," she sobbed, "Amanda and Sallie are missing."

"No, they aren't. We just took them home, along with Joe," John told her, smoothing her soft, blonde hair.

"Thank the Lord!" Elizabeth cried.

When John explained what had happened, the women were joyous, eager to get back to the house. Tsa'ni said nothing.

As they started back to Uncle Ned's house, by way of the hospital site, Tsa'ni took the lead, carrying the lighted lantern. When they came around the corner of the hospital, they almost tripped over Running Fire and his two sons, who were dozing under a nearby tree in the darkness.

Startled, the three troublesome Indians grabbed their guns and jumped to their feet.

Uncle John and Uncle Ned quickly stepped in front of the women and drew their rifles. Everyone was silent, waiting for the other to make the first move.

"We know all about you," Uncle John warned the three.

"Drop gun or we shoot!" Uncle Wirt yelled at them.

Running Fire took one step forward. "*You* drop gun or *we* shoot," he snarled.

Uncle Ned's eyes flashed with anger. "You, Catawba man, drop that gun. Cherokees all about in woods."

Tsa'ni quietly slipped behind a tree trunk and blew out the lantern. In the pitch-black darkness he quickly jumped on top of Running Fire.

The other men realized what he was doing, and also made a dive for the strangers. The Catawba men were outnumbered, and Uncle Ned's party soon had them under control. As Uncle Wirt quickly tied their hands, Dimar took their rifles.

Uncle John approached Running Fire.

The Catawba man cringed.

"Do not touch me, white man!" he yelled. "I am Running Fire, the medicine man for all Catawbas."

"I know who you are," Uncle John replied. "And I won't touch you. You're too filthy for me to dirty my hands on. But let me tell you this. If you and your family are not long gone by sunup, you will wish you were. Every Cherokee in the nation will be hunting you. And they will do more serious things to you than we are."

"Dirty crook!" Uncle Ned spat at the old man. "Hurt doctor boy. Hide Papooses."

Uncle Wirt shook his big hands at them. "You here sunup I take you apart."

Dimar spoke up. "And I will help. I am young and I am strong."

Tsa'ni stood silently listening. Then he stepped forward and pushed the three strangers.

"Get! Now!" he yelled at them.

The Catawbas, anxiously glancing behind them, ran through the woods with their hands still tied together and disappeared.

Uncle John turned to Uncle Ned and asked, "Do you think they will leave?"

"If they do not leave, we make them leave," Uncle Ned assured him. "Must get message to other Cherokees now to watch and see they leave. Also tell Cherokees Joe found."

"I will spread the word," Dimar offered.

Tsa'ni stepped forward, saying, "And I will help."

Everyone turned in surprise. Tsa'ni was finally volunteering. The two boys hurried off into the woods on their mission.

Uncle Ned, Uncle Wirt and Uncle John trudged back through the woods to Uncle Ned's house, with the women carefully surrounded.

What would they find at Uncle Ned's house? Would Joe be all right? Would anyone else have disappeared?

Chapter 13 / Tomorrow . . .

Dr. Woodard was still sitting beside Joe's bed when the others returned. Mandie and Sallie sat nearby on the floor. They jumped when Uncle Ned knocked on the door.

"Let us in," he called. "We home."

The girls raced to the door and removed the crossbar. Mandie ran to her mother's arms while Sallie embraced her grandmother.

As they all gathered around the warm fire, the men told how they had met Running Fire and his sons in the woods and ordered them to leave Cherokee territory, and the girls related their adventures to Elizabeth and Morning Star.

Suddenly, in the midst of the excitement, Joe opened his eyes. "What's going on?" he asked weakly.

Everyone gathered around his bed, grateful that he had regained consciousness.

His father gripped his hand and smiled. "Well, it's like this, son. We brought you back here to Uncle Ned's house, the crooks have been caught, and everything seems to be under control," said Dr. Woodard, wiping the perspiration from his brow.

Mandie ran over to Joe, knelt by the bed, and took his hand. "Oh, Joe!" she cried. "I'm so glad you're getting well."

Joe smiled at her. "I have to get well," he said in a stronger voice. "Remember, we're going to get married when we get grown."

Tears welled up in Mandie's eyes, and she buried her face in the covers.

Joe patted her blonde head. "Now, please get me some food, woman. I'm hungry. And not any of that owl stew stuff either," Joe teased.

"Now I know you're better!" Mandie cried. Getting to her feet, she went to see what Morning Star had cooked that day.

Morning Star had understood Joe's request and was already ladling soup from the big black iron pot into a bowl. She handed it to Mandie with a smile. Mandie took it and hurried back to the bed.

"Can you sit up to eat this?" she asked.

"No, you're going to have to feed me," Joe said with a sly grin.

His father looked at him disapprovingly. "Now, Joe, come on," he said. "I'll prop you up on the pillows. Here." He smiled as he tried to make the bed more comfortable.

"I'll hold the bowl," Mandie offered. "You use the spoon and eat this good soup."

Joe propped himself up on one elbow and began to eat the soup slowly. He seemed to revive as the hot broth went down. When he had eaten all he could, he moved a little to stretch. "Oh, I'm sore!" he said. "Those men beat me up."

"We know," said Uncle John, "but they won't be bothering you or anyone else around here. They were ordered out of the territory and the Cherokees are all watching to make sure they leave."

Everyone joined in a garbled explanation of what had happened since the Catawba men took Joe.

Joe was furious when he heard that Mandie and Sallie had also been kidnapped. "It's good they will be gone by the time I can get out of this bed. I'd like to take care of them myself," he said.

Just then Tsa'ni and Dimar came in, having relayed their message to the other Cherokees.

When Mandie saw Tsa'ni, she knew she had to ease her guilty conscience. Embarrassed, she slowly walked over to him. "Tsa'ni, I must beg your forgiveness," she began, clearing her throat nervously. She never knew what reaction she would get from the Indian boy.

"For what?" Tsa'ni asked sullenly.

"I wrongly accused you of tearing down the hospital walls and of knowing where Joe was. I know now that I was wrong, very wrong. I'm sorry, Tsa'ni. I ask you to forgive me," she said.

The others listened silently.

"You will get your hospital built," Tsa'ni replied. "I know now that the hospital is necessary for the advancement of the Cherokees. We must catch up with and pass the white man. For many, many years the Cherokees have been held back and had no chance to improve. No more. The hospital will be built," Tsa'ni declared.

"But, Tsa'ni, will you forgive me?" Mandie repeated.

"Accusations of the white man do not matter to me because—" Tsa'ni paused. He hung his head and then straightened up to look Mandie in the eye. "I cannot be angry with you because, after all, you are my cousin. I am sorry, too." He grinned and held out his hand.

Mandie gripped his hand tightly and looked upward. *Dear God*, she prayed silently, *please forgive me.* Looking back at Tsa'ni, she smiled. "Thank you, Tsa'ni, for forgiving me. I love you, my cousin."

Tsa'ni stuck his hand in his pocket and sauntered off to the other side of the room.

Uncle Ned put his arm around Mandie's shoulders and steered her to another corner of the room. "Papoose must think with head," he said softly. "Think before Papoose does things. Over and over Papoose do something then think. Backward way. Must think first. Must remember. Think first. Think first."

Mandie reached up to grasp his hand on her shoulder. "I will try, Uncle Ned. I will try real hard," she promised.

"Big Book say not judge," the old Indian reminded her.

"I know. 'Judge not, that ye be not judged,' " she quoted the Bible verse. "I'm going to do my best, and I hope you'll help me," she said, smiling up at him.

"I help," said Uncle Ned. "I promise Jim Shaw I watch over Papoose when he go to happy hunting ground. I keep promise."

"I love you, Uncle Ned," said Mandie as they embraced.

A few minutes later, Mandie turned her attention back to Joe and his father. "Dr. Woodard, how long will it take Joe to recover?" she asked.

"He should be well enough to go home in a day or two," the doctor replied.

"Oh, that's wonderful!" said Mandie. Relieved that Joe was going to be all right, she looked over at her mother and Uncle John. "Can we still go to Charleston?" she asked hopefully.

"I don't see any reason why we can't leave first thing in the morning," Uncle John replied.

Mandie could hardly contain her excitement. At last she would get to see the great big ocean!

Cooking with Mandie!

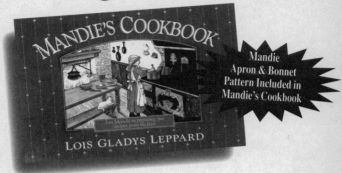

*A*fter days and days of begging, Mandie finally convinced Aunt Lou to teach her how to cook. You know who Aunt Lou is—Mandie's Uncle John's Housekeeper. Mandie not only loved learning how to cook, but she recorded every recipe, every "do" and "don't" that they went through. And that is how this cookbook came to be.

Mandie also learned how to cook Cherokee-style from Morning Star, Uncle Ned's wife. Sallie, her granddaughter, helped translate since Morning Star doesn't speak English. Being part Cherokee, Mandie wanted to learn how her kin-people cook.

With Mandie's step-by-step instructions, you can cook and serve meals and share the experiences of girls from the turn of the century. Learn how to bake cakes and pies, do popcorn balls, make biscuits and Southern fried chicken, as well as make Indian recipes like dried apples and potato skins.

If you love the Mandie Books, you'll love to try cooking Mandie's favorite recipes!

Series for Middle Graders*
From Bethany House Publishers

ADVENTURES DOWN UNDER · by Robert Elmer
When Patrick McWaid's father is unjustly sent to Australia as a prisoner in 1867, the rest of the family follows, uncovering action-packed mystery along the way.

ADVENTURES OF THE NORTHWOODS · by Lois Walfrid Johnson
Kate O'Connell and her stepbrother Anders encounter mystery and adventure in northwest Wisconsin near the turn of the century.

AN AMERICAN ADVENTURE SERIES · by Lee Roddy
Hildy Corrigan and her family must overcome danger and hardship during the Great Depression as they search for a "forever home."

BLOODHOUNDS, INC. · by Bill Myers
Hilarious, hair-raising suspense follows brother-and-sister detectives Sean and Melissa Hunter in these madcap mysteries with a message.

JOURNEYS TO FAYRAH · by Bill Myers
Join Denise, Nathan, and Josh on amazing journeys as they discover the wonders and lessons of the mystical Kingdom of Fayrah.

MANDIE BOOKS · by Lois Gladys Leppard
With over four million sold, the turn-of-the-century adventures of Mandie and her many friends will keep readers eager for more.

THE RIVERBOAT ADVENTURES · by Lois Walfrid Johnson
Libby Norstad and her friend Caleb face the challenges and risks of working with the Underground Railroad during the mid–1800s.

TRAILBLAZER BOOKS · by Dave and Neta Jackson
Follow the exciting lives of real-life Christian heroes through the eyes of child characters as they share their faith and God's love with others around the world.

THE TWELVE CANDLES CLUB · by Elaine L. Schulte
When four twelve-year-old girls set up a business doing odd jobs and baby-sitting, they find themselves in the midst of wacky adventures and hilarious surprises.

THE YOUNG UNDERGROUND · by Robert Elmer
Peter and Elise Andersen's plots to protect their friends and themselves from Nazi soldiers in World War II Denmark guarantee fast-paced action and suspenseful reads.

*(ages 8–13)